DIAMOND QUEEN

SHANON L. MAYER

DIAMOND QUEEN

SHADOW TRIBUNAL,
BOOK 1

Shanon Mayer

First Printing, 2023

Cover design by JD&J Design
ISBN: 978-1-958076-14-9
Published by Shanon L. Mayer, Vancouver WA 98663

https://shanonlmayer.com

This is for everyone who told me that I couldn't write in a science fiction world and to stay in my own lane. Thanks for the encouragement, it was exactly what I needed!

CONTENTS

1 — The Blind Bird
1

2 — The Fire Exhibit
12

3 — Insecure Storage
19

4 — Suited for Exile
26

5 — Know your Enemy
33

6 — A Basket of Fruit
41

7 — The Shimmer in the Desert
48

8 — Familiar Territory
59

9 — Calling all Cards
64

10 — The Despair of Futility
71

CONTENTS

11 — A Rock, a Hard Place, and a Psionist
80

12 — Very Special Delivery
90

13 — Home Away from Home Away from Home
98

14 — Dishonor among Thieves
103

15 — Meeting of the Minds
110

16 — Enemy of My Enemy
123

17 — Mouth of the Lion
128

18 — Terros Sweet Terros
135

19 — Signus IV
140

20 — The Collection Agency
145

21 — Slow Growth
148

22 — Kill Orders
157

23 — Growing Pains
163

CONTENTS

24 — Tico's Nightmare
170

25 — Survival Instincts
180

26 — Broken Promise
185

27 — Midway General
190

28 — Bringing the Battle to Them
198

29 — Power Source
208

30 — The Submarine Thief
213

31 — Assault on Cardiss
221

32 — All the King's Men
228

33 — Silent Base
234

BOOKS BY SHANON L. MAYER

Chronicles of the Chosen
Sphere of Power
Veil of Deception
Reflections of Doubt

Jen Rice novels
Captives and Prisoners
Festival of Souls
Beautiful Monsters

Inland Sea
Star of Darkness
Eyes of Midnight

Shadow Tribunal
Diamond Queen

THE BLIND BIRD

"I like this one."

"Really?" Thomas Ranger leaned over to see what his partner was pointing at. "Don't you already have something like that?" His honey-colored hair drifted down in front of his eyes as he leaned, accentuating rather than obscuring his sharply defined features.

Thomas was slightly more than two units tall, which was roughly seven feet in this region's measuring system, average height for the region he originally hailed from but much taller than average for Portland, Oregon, where he and Michelle had chosen to make their home. He ran a thoughtful hand through his hair, noting that it was overdue for a trim.

He wasn't heavily muscled, although he could easily have become as sculpted as a professional bodybuilder or fitness model. Instead, he kept himself toned and trim, careful to moderate the amount of bulk he packed on. His height alone brought far more attention than he wanted, his glower even more so. Thick, dark brows set in a heavy forehead cast shadows over his eyes, making them look slightly sunken and giving him an overall brooding appearance regardless of his mood.

Michelle Deva looked back down at the brochure in her hands, lips pursed but unbothered by his expression. A small bronze-cast bird teased her imagination from the page they were both looking at. Although it was obvious that the bird had once held gems or other such treasures in its eyes, both of the sockets had been blinded by time. The figure was small, even if the photograph wasn't life-sized, and she couldn't tell whether it was a sparrow, a robin, or a starling.

The metal itself appeared slightly worn, though not as much as others of similar style that she had come across in the past. There were a couple of substantial scratches running the length of the bird's body, but rather than devaluing the piece in Michelle's eyes, the blemishes only added to the statue's character. Even if it was blind, the bird had obviously seen much.

"I don't have one of these," she answered after a contemplative moment. "I have a stork."

"Isn't a stork a bird?"

Michelle nodded. "A stork may be a bird, but this," she lifted the brochure from her lap and waved it in the air absently, "is not a stork." She unfolded her impossibly long legs, made to appear even longer due to the barely-present skirt tied around her waist, and stood to pace across the room.

"Isn't it missing a couple eyes there?"

"Just gems," she responded without looking up. "Those are easy enough to replace." Although she wasn't sure which type of gemstone was originally in the metallic figurine, there were plenty to choose from to replace the missing stones. Garnets, perhaps, or maybe rubies. Perhaps emeralds or even sapphires. Her eyes glinted as she considered the possibilities. Her favorite thing about gemstones, as anyone who spent time around her quickly discovered, was the sheer array of colors they came in.

Unlike Thomas's disheveled appearance, Michelle could have been the poster child for personal grooming. She spent over an hour in the bathroom each morning before Thomas woke, winding her wavy, golden blonde hair into one of her many thousands of pairs of hair sticks and shaping the remaining strands to frame the style. Meticulously applied makeup ensured that, unless one looked very closely, her skin was flawless and her age was almost completely undeterminable. More importantly, the faint red markings that ran down her arms and legs were all but invisible.

Most people were caught by her intricate hair or her shapely legs but were truly ensnared by her eyes. Thick, brown lashes surrounded a pair of enormous emerald eyes with flecks of gold beckoning attention to the center. Some explained her fascinating eyes as a trick of her makeup, a styling tip that almost everyone she met wanted to learn.

Those people would never believe that the makeup she applied so carefully each morning made her eyes look not larger, as everyone believed, but smaller than they truly were. Where Thomas's physical stature was an anomaly in their current location but not completely unheard-of, her eye size was far outside the range of normal human proportions.

Thomas just shrugged at Michelle's explanation. One type of bird statue was the same as another, according to him. He would never understand how Michelle was able to discern the difference between the types of birds; there were about a million varieties across the planet, all of which looked the same in his opinion. Not that the argument mattered. It was one that they frequently rehashed, at least once every couple of months. The only difference was the item in question and whether it had caught Thomas's attention or Michelle's. They both knew that whatever they wanted from the exhibit, as long as it was within reach, it would be in their possession before they were done, one way or another.

If Michelle wanted the bird, whatever kind it was, he would help her get it.

The Portland Art Museum, located in the heart of the city of Portland, was one of the largest cultural museums in the Pacific Northwest. The previous week, the museum proprietors had announced an upcoming exhibit of priceless Phoenician and Egyptian artifacts, starting at the beginning of the following month. For three weeks, some of the most spectacular examples of the enigmatic history of the Middle East would be displayed for all who paid a nominal entrance fee to enter. The brochures that Thomas and Michelle were poring over included a listing of some of the more interesting and crowd-appealing pieces, meant to draw more people - and therefore more funds - to the museum during the exhibit.

Photographs of hundreds of items filled the brochure pages, from a golden lion's-head medallion to statues of people that were almost life-sized to decorative pottery and vessels made of gold or bronze. Many of the pieces were worn almost smooth from age but Michelle wasn't interested in these. Although she didn't mind a little bit of character in the pieces she selected for her personal collection, the pieces she selected had to be immediately recognizable. She didn't want to have to make the argument that it was more than just a chunk of rock, which was precisely what quite a few of the items in the catalog appeared to be, despite their historical value. There weren't many pieces listed in the brochure that Michelle *hadn't* said she wanted. It didn't matter whether she already had something similar; a stork from the Xang dynasty was not the same as this tiny, sculpted Phoenician bird.

"Do we know how they're going to be moving the artifacts to and from the museum yet?" she asked as she turned from the page with the bird to a different page she had marked, one with tiny figures of warriors in battle dress. She wasn't completely certain that she wanted the human figures, but she had to admit an amount of attraction to them.

Thomas scanned through a stack of documents on the low table before the couch, papers which were comprised mostly of surveillance that the pair of them had put together. Photographs, time schedules, and pages filled with carefully hand-written notes were interspersed among pages of research printed from the internet and other, less legal, sources. As soon as they discovered the exhibit would be arriving, Michelle and Thomas began learning all they could about the exhibit, its sponsors, and the museum at which it would be on display.

"Looks like they're going to be using Christopherson Transport," he answered without looking up from the pages. "No big surprise there." He picked a transcript from the middle of the stack, one of many copies that their surveillance system had made of all the museum office's phone calls.

No big surprise, indeed. As far as Michelle could tell, it would have been far more of a surprise if the museum had decided to use anyone other than Christopherson Transport. She stopped pacing and turned to face him. "Have they already scheduled the delivery?"

"Of course. From what I've got here, it looks like they'll be spending the week before the exhibit shuttling everything into town."

"That could be a problem." Her lips twisted into a pouting frown. If the exhibit would take an entire week to ship, then getting everything in one nice, neatly bundled package would prove difficult.

Thomas didn't answer; he just nodded and continued to scan his pages. Occasionally he would lean forward to grasp his mug of tea and take a drink, swirling the lightly sweetened warmth across his tongue before setting the cup back down again. It didn't matter how long they had lived in the Pacific Northwest, or how much the locals screamed about how wonderful their coffee was, he had never developed a taste for the bitter black brew.

Tea had been his drink of choice since their arrival in Oregon and, as far as he was concerned, tea would remain such for the foreseeable future. Thankfully, although coffee was far more in vogue than other beverages, aside from those horrid energy drinks that even a cockroach would turn an antenna up at, there was a wide selection of local teas for him to amass a collection of as well. That had been done quite successfully as the assortment of tins, boxes, and pouches scattered throughout the kitchen cupboards could attest.

"I think we should set a fire." Unnoticed, Michelle had taken her seat on the couch next to him once more.

Her words interrupted his musing and almost caused him to spill his Darjeeling onto the rug. Not that anyone would notice if he had spilled the tea; the rug was a hideous abstract abomination in browns, reds, oranges and greens that he hated. The stain would blend right in as though it belonged there.

"What?"

"A fire," she repeated. "Right here." While he had been reading, she had pulled out the floor plan of the museum and unrolled it next to the rest of the papers, using a handful of small paperweights to hold it flat. Now, she pointed to one of the rooms in the southeast corner of the building. She sat back and tucked her feet beneath her, resuming the pose she had been in when he had first entered the room.

"That would be counterproductive," he said as he settled his mug onto the table and set his own stack of papers next to it. "If we burn everything, there won't be anything left over for us."

"I didn't say we were going to burn everything," she said, exasperation washing over him with every syllable. "I said we should set a fire."

"I know you haven't lost your mind," he said as he looked from the blueprint to his companion. "I also know you wouldn't really intend to destroy all of these priceless antiques."

His words were bland, but the question was obvious. Or perhaps not so obvious, he realized as her eyes continued to bore a hole through him.

"We can't set a fire in the museum," he argued. "First of all, there are too many things there that we can't risk destroying." He lowered his brow at her as he took another sip of his tea. That expression, coupled with his calculating brown eyes, so dark they looked black in all but the brightest of lights, and thick, heavy brows, led many to believe that he was always angry – a trait he wasn't above exploiting when the need arose.

Michelle had known him too long to fall for such tactics. "Nope, we won't destroy anything," she agreed. "That would be pretty pointless." A smile slowly grew across her face as she spoke.

Okay, so maybe she did have a plan. He hated it when she made him play the guessing game, but he knew she wouldn't tell him anything more unless he played along. "What about security?" he countered. "Cameras, door alarms, motion sensors, and individual exhibit alarms." He took another sip of the tea before settling the cup back onto the table. "Sure, we can get past those, but it would take all night and not leave us any time to get anything out of it." He met her unblinking stare. "Plus," he added, "There's the fire department to think of. We both know that the museum's pretty high priority, so they'll be there before we got through very far at all."

She considered his arguments for a moment before rebutting them. "The fire department will be there, of course. After all, someone's got to save all the antiques from the fire."

She leaned forward and stole his half-full cup, taking a drink and grimacing before setting it back down. "Why do you have to drink that stuff?" She complained about the tea, as she always did. "With all of the herbals in the cupboard, why do you have to drink the blacks?

"And security won't get in our way." Her grimace melted into a dazzling grin. "In fact, if they even notice us, I'll be amazed."

Despite her certainty, Thomas wasn't sure she had countered any of his arguments, but she seemed to be far too sure of herself to be easily dismissed. "Do you really think that security's going to just let us walk in, grab what we want, and then walk out with it?" He chuckled at the idea. "I never realized you were completely daft."

"We won't steal their exhibit." She shook her head, a pair of long curls bouncing appealingly as she moved. "We wait until after the exhibit closes."

"And then start a fire."

"Here." Finally, he looked more closely at where she was pointing, and saw the wisdom in her suggestion. Although he hadn't immediately made the connection, their earlier trips to the museum had shown both of them that one of the rooms was currently being used for, and would continue for the next six months, a display of fossilized dinosaur bones and tracks. She had immediately dubbed it the Stone Room, and if anywhere could be said to be a good place to set a fire in the museum, the Stone Room would be it.

He nodded, agreeing with her assessment. "So how do we get the goods out?"

"With trucks." She settled back against the arm of the couch and tucked one of the curls behind an ear. "Everyone will be panicking over the fire and they'll want to get their precious artifacts out as fast as they can. Since we're going to wait until after the show's over, they'll already be packing it up and getting it ready to go.

"All we have to do is make them rush."

Thomas pursed his lips, trying to decide whether he liked her plan. It was genius in its simplicity, he had to admit. An added bonus was that they already had a van that matched the ones used by Christopherson in storage. They had planned to use it in a previous heist but it had proven unnecessary. Now, maybe, their investment wouldn't be a complete waste after all.

"It has the added benefit of distraction," he agreed. "They'll be so focused on putting out the fire and keeping it from spreading into the rest of the museum, they'll be less likely to be paying that close attention to the loading of our exhibit."

"I do love a good distraction," she agreed. "You wait out in the truck," Michelle continued to unfold her plan. "Down the street, around the block; we'll figure out exactly where it'll be later. I will be inside and in place when the alarms start to go off, so I can help direct which crates go into which truck."

"And how do you plan to do that?" It wasn't that he doubted she could do it; half the time, all she had to do was walk into a room for all of the attention to be on her. Even if people didn't quite understand why they were doing it, they instinctively reacted to her presence and wanted to please her. He still wasn't sure whether it was something that she did intentionally or if it was just an aspect of her existence that couldn't be helped.

"I'll just make sure I'm up on volunteer rotation that day." She had been an occasional volunteer at the museum for the last five months, so her presence wouldn't be suspicious. "I can set up the timed explosives to go off at, say, three thirty. Then, when it's about time, I can be on the loading dock, ready to do my part and help save the priceless artifacts."

She looked so serious as she said the last part that Thomas almost felt sorry for anyone who dared suspect her. Not that they would, he realized. They never did. Michelle's air of innocence, one that constantly surrounded her even when she wasn't trying to project it, had been the downfall of far too many people for him to not recognize its power. One thing that she had learned quickly was that the people of this world appeared to equate beauty and charm with innocence, so that people who presented as young, attractive and well put-together citizens were almost completely beyond reproach. The day she learned that nuance of society was the day she bought almost the entire beauty counter from the local department store and began perfecting her makeup, hair and wardrobe. Her size also played into the perception of innocence as she was positively tiny compared to most of the people she interacted with on a regular basis.

When she *tried* to appear sweet and innocent, however, was when she was truly dangerous.

"So how does this keep everything from being destroyed?" He asked after another long moment. "I get what you're saying, but even a fire started in the Stone Room will spread out to other areas fairly quickly. How do you expect to contain it?"

"We won't have to," she explained as he continued to think. "It can be more smoke than fire; that's easy enough to do." She smiled at him. "Just enough to convince them that there *is* a fire. I'm sure it wouldn't take you any time at all to put something together."

"Nope," he said as he took his cup away from her before she could drink any more of it. Thankfully, it had cooled enough that he could actually drink it this time, so he took another sip for the pure pleasure of it. "Won't take long at all."

It really wouldn't; he had a handful of smoke bombs made already, so augmenting them for the museum job would be simplicity in itself.

They spent the next few weeks finalizing their plans and gathering all of the supplies they would need. Thomas checked on the van that they would use to haul away their bounty and added the graphics that would make it indistinguishable from the legitimate transportation vans. Michelle batted a perfectly-shaped eyelash at the volunteer supervisor and he was more than willing to offer her whichever shifts she wanted.

The plan was perfect. Their escape would be brilliant. Their rendezvous after it was all completed would be completely unnoticed by anyone.

It was perfect.

THE FIRE EXHIBIT

As Michelle pulled into the parking lot where she was to meet up with Thomas, she reflected back on the success of the heist. Everything had gone off precisely as planned. In fact, in a few small ways, it had gone even better than either of them could have hoped.

She selected a spot far enough away from the building to be out of the way of shoppers but angled so that she had a clear view of the brightly-lit supermarket and both of the cross streets that ran past it. There had not been any major surprises yet and she wasn't interested in discovering something unexpected sneaking up on her now. She turned off the van and settled down to wait for Thomas, certain that she wouldn't have to wait long.

It had been laughably easy to convince Vinnie Mendoza, the volunteer coordinator, to schedule her for the shift she wanted. The only difficulty there had been in sidestepping his interest in asking her out on a date again. As useful as her friendship with Vinnie had been, she wasn't interested in anything further.

Placing the bombs she had requested into an exhibit in the Stone Room had been just as simple. Instead of the timed explosion like she had originally envisioned, the compact tubular devices Thomas assembled for the afternoon's diversion were connected to the same remote trigger that would alert both her and Thomas when it was armed. That had allowed her to place the explosives the day before the heist, while security was busy overseeing the packaging of the Egyptian exhibit. The fact that each of them, despite the amount of explosive material within them, was less than a tenth of a unit in length just made it that much easier to conceal them.

When the alarms sounded, alerting the museum staff and visitors alike that there was a problem, Michelle made her way quietly to the loading dock. "What's going on?" she demanded of the first person she saw. She wasn't familiar with the man she addressed, although his uniform and name badge indicated he worked for the museum. Three Christopherson vans already filled some of the loading dock.

"Fire," he grunted, given with barely more than a glance in her direction. "We need to get these crates out of here, fast."

Michelle stepped into the thick of the action. Dozens of crates were scattered around the staging area, each sealed box containing the valuable artifacts that had been carefully displayed only the day before. They all looked almost identical, but her eyes went immediately to the crates that she had marked the day before. Those three crates contained the artifacts that she and Thomas had decided to take, so as long as she got them loaded into Thomas's van, everything would be perfectly according to plan.

Sirens sounded in the distance as the fire department reacted to the alarms. Michelle glanced quickly at the watch on her wrist and checked the time. Right on schedule. Also right on schedule was the fourth loading bay opening to allow another van into the chaos.

As the bay opened, a van backed into the available spot. Although it was indistinguishable from the other vans, she knew that Thomas was the only person inside. She called one of the loaders over to her and pointed at a crate. "Get that in truck four," she said as she pulled the loading papers from a clipboard and slapped the transport sticker onto the crate. She had to shout to be heard over the cacophony of everyone barking loading orders for the artifacts.

The young man didn't hesitate. He pulled a pallet jack from nearby and shoved it beneath the crate.

"These ones, too." Michelle stepped quickly and with authority down the line of crates she already considered to be hers, attaching loading stickers onto each as she went to ensure they were loaded into the correct vehicle. "Let's get these things moving!" The scent of smoke filled the air as the doors leading into the building were opened and closed again.

Leaving the loader to his work, she went from crate to crate, assigning some for loading into the available vans and sending the transports out as they were filled. Nobody challenged her authority. *It's amazing*, she thought to herself, *how effective of a disguise a clipboard and the impression you know what you're doing can be.*

When the first man she had grabbed to start loading her van returned but moved for a different stack of crates, she sprinted to catch up with him. "What are you doing?" she demanded. "There's still a crate to load."

He thumbed over at another of the loaders, this one a supervisor. "He said this one needed to go next. Since that truck's ready to go, he wants it out now."

Michelle swore under her breath. She had no idea what was in the crate but, as she watched it settle into place in the van, she had to quell the anger as it rose in her. She had hand-selected which items she wanted and one of her favorites, the tiny, gilded bird, was in the crate that was being left behind.

She calmed quickly, trying to come up with another plan on the fly. The number of cases was swiftly diminishing, so she didn't have long to decide.

More sirens came screaming into the museum's periphery and Michelle wondered at the amount of response. She hadn't expected quite this many emergency vehicles to arrive but the chaos they brought with them only served to make her life easier. At least, as far as stealing the crates filled with artifacts went.

"Not that one," she stopped one of the loaders, not the same man she had already sent to retrieve the crate. She pointed at another nearby crate. "Take that one, and then the one next to it."

Slowly, all of the cases but the one she wanted were loaded into the waiting vans and taken away to be moved to their next destination. When there was only one truck left, she had the crate placed inside. "I'll ride with it," she called over to the handful of people who were left in the bay as she hooked her clipboard onto one of the already-loaded crates. "You guys better get out too," she flashed her million-watt grin at the loaders. "The building's on fire."

One of the loaders chuckled as he closed the doors behind her and Michelle let the painfully wide grin fade to a small smile of satisfaction, thankful that she could finally slip out of her harried façade. She knew that she would get everything she came for, she realized as she looked around the cargo space. She just hadn't expected to get even more than that. She braced herself between a crate and the wall of the cargo area as the van bounced out of the loading area and turned onto the street. "Easy now," she muttered quietly. "These things are valuable." Once the van was steadily moving on the street, she began to maneuver forward.

"Like I said," she muttered to herself as she crawled over crates on her way up to the passenger area of the van. "Fire." She dropped into the passenger seat without bothering with the safety belt and smiled at her erstwhile driver. "Thanks for the ride."

The driver was a nice-looking boy, in his late twenties if Michelle had to guess. He had dark brown hair peeking out from beneath his uniform hat and friendly hazel eyes. If he was surprised that she had joined him for the ride, he didn't let it show in his expression. "No problem," he returned her smile. "Twizzler?"

They chatted amicably about nothing memorable for about fifteen minutes as they drove toward the airport. On one hand, Michelle knew that she could easily get away with all that she and Thomas had taken in his van simply by continuing to act as a passenger until their arrival at the airport but there was no way that she was going to leave this last crate behind. She didn't want to run the risk of leaving her precious bird, the item that had initially drawn her to the exhibit in the first place, behind after all of the effort she had put in to secure it for her personal collection.

It was just too bad that the driver was in the way. He seemed like such a nice kid. In any other circumstance, she probably would have liked him. She'd never had Twizzlers before and wasn't too keen on the texture, but they tasted alright and she accepted another when it was offered.

When they stopped at a red light partway to their destination, Michelle pulled a small tube from her pocket. It was pen-shaped, or at least would have been if pens were four times the size of their regular diameter. While the pen worked as any other pen would, its true usefulness was located in the tiny button near the bottom, away from the ink.

Thomas had been so proud the day he gave it to her. "You're out by yourself too often," he had told her as he handed it over. "This can help me sleep a little better at night, knowing that you're safe."

They both knew she hadn't needed the weapon to ensure her safety, or any weapon for that matter, and until the day of the heist her partner had been the only person she had ever used it on. It released a concentrated beam of electricity when the button was depressed, much like a low-powered taser. When used on the fleshy areas of the body, the beam wasn't enough to stop or even really hurt anybody for long, but she had quickly discovered that if she pressed the tip to the spine, particularly at the base of the skull, it would render her target unconscious.

Thomas hadn't known about that when he gave her the device but, once she discovered the trick, he had warned her exactly what he would do if she ever did that to him again.

She moved the now-unconscious driver to the passenger seat and turned left at the next intersection, careful to follow all of the traffic laws. The last thing she needed was to draw suspicion on her now. After a few more turns, just to be sure that there wasn't anyone physically following her, she slowly began to make her way to the small storage unit where she and Thomas kept some of their discoveries, at least until a suitable buyer could be found.

Thomas was already in the process of unloading their van when she arrived. Michelle, not wanting to lead the authorities to their hiding place on the off chance that there was an electronic monitor on the van she drove, maintained her course but waved to him as she passed.

She pulled into the parking lot of a local supermarket, one that they had used plenty of times before and where they knew no cameras could record their movements. Only a handful of customers wandered in and out of the store and none of the employees could see through the windows facing them because of all the advertising paraphernalia that was plastered across the glass. Nobody paid any attention to the green and yellow van parked on the outer edge of the parking lot.

Soon after turning off the ignition, an identical van pulled in next to her, turned around, and backed up so that the cargo could be unloaded directly from one van into the next.

"I had to," she answered his unspoken question. "A couple of the crates got switched, so one of ours is in here." She beamed up at him. "Besides, this means we got double the take."

Both of the vans had to be disposed of. The one that she had taken needed to disappear for obvious reasons; neither of them wanted the authorities to use it to locate their hiding place. As for the one they already had, Thomas always insisted on the disposal of a vehicle once it had been used in a heist. "Just in case there's a mark on it that we didn't notice but someone else did," he explained for the millionth time, "we can't risk using anything more than once."

She mouthed silently along as he rambled about tracking devices and laser identification systems, some of which they knew were available to law enforcement and some of which they didn't want to take any chances about finding out too late that they had.

The unconscious driver of Michelle's van wouldn't be a problem. He never woke up as they moved him onto a bus stop bench, and he was blissfully unaware as the van with which he had been entrusted burned in phosphorous-enhanced glory two towns over.

INSECURE STORAGE

When they returned to their home that evening, pleased with the success of the day, Thomas drove straight past the squat, yellow-sided house without stopping.

"Forget where you're going?" Michelle chided him, but her words were without malice. Thomas had a perfect map of their neighborhood, their town, and many of the surrounding towns in his head, so there was no possibility of him losing his way, especially as he drove down their own street.

In response, he pulled his cell phone out of his shirt pocket and tossed it into her lap. It was buzzing and for a brief moment she wondered who would be texting him. When she flipped it open, however, she discovered that the vibration was far more important than any text message could be. "Perimeter Security Breach," the message flashed on the small screen.

Michelle's mind raced through all of the different locations where she knew he had put alarm systems in and briefly wondered which place had been discovered. Only as she was about to ask, however, did she realize the obvious truth. "Someone's in our house?"

He grunted and turned onto another maple-lined street before answering. "Not in the house. That's the alarm to the storage unit." He stopped at the sign at the end of the block, turn signal flashing on the dashboard as he waited for the crossing traffic to clear.

Michelle sat back, stunned. It couldn't have been more than fifteen minutes since they had been there. "Are you sure?"

Of course he was sure and the question didn't really require an answer. Both of them knew that the security and warning systems that Thomas put up everywhere wouldn't send him a message such as the one he had received unless there really was a problem. "Are we headed back to see what happened?"

"Nope." He turned another corner, and she realized that they had made a complete circuit of their neighborhood. "Looks like that's all they found, though."

"But how?" the question wasn't really directed at Thomas. Although Michelle had asked the question, they both knew the answer. Somehow the van she had taken had led the authorities to them. Perhaps someone had placed a tracker into one of the crates in the second van without her knowledge. She had been careful to ensure no tracking devices were in any of the originally targeted crates, but since she had never intended to take the extras, she hadn't paid any attention to what was being put in with the artifacts. A simple mistake, and hers alone.

"House is safe," he reassured her as he turned into the driveway. "No warnings, no security breaches, and there's nobody loitering about that doesn't belong here."

Reassured but by no means relieved, she hopped out of the car and headed for the house, Thomas not far behind. Ignoring the flashing light on the answering machine and the empty cup where Thomas had apparently left his drink from that morning, they headed to the back hallway. As with most of the house, the walls were decorated in two parts: a painted upper section, the colors carefully selected to complement whatever decorations had been placed nearby, with whitewashed vertical slats of wood beneath the painted section to add a rustic touch. On the wall of this part of their home, where very few visitors were allowed, replicas of Van Gogh's *Sunflowers* and *Starry Night* dominated the beige wall, with a half-unit-wide empty space between them.

She placed her hand directly beneath *Starry Night*, pressing her palm securely against the caramel-colored surface. There was nothing on the wall to show where her hand needed to be placed or what would happen when it was, but she knew exactly what she was doing. From beneath the thin coating of paint directly next to her hand, a tiny red light blinked three times in rapid succession before turning green and disappearing. She let go of the wall as, with barely a whisper of friction, the wall slipped down into the hidden recess behind the wooden panels.

Computer monitors and keyboards dominated the revealed space, with flashing red, blue, and orange lights calling their attention everywhere. With a flick of a switch, a holographic map of the town appeared above the display and there was a glaring red brightness where the silence of their storage area should have been.

Thomas swore and flipped a pair of switches, which turned on the monitors. They flashed to life and flickered for a moment before displaying the images captured by the hidden cameras he had installed before any contraband had been moved into the holding rooms.

Seven men and women moved through the wide space, sometimes obscured behind the crates that had just arrived, others walking boldly down the paths that Thomas and Michelle had left open for maneuverability. They quickly identified the man in charge, and Michelle joined Thomas in swearing.

"Isn't that deVann?" she asked among expletives. When Thomas made no response, she swore again. She had known the truth but hoped that she was somehow mistaken.

Lucas deVann was a member of the FBI, which was bad enough. Six years ago, a task force had been activated with the goal of stopping the rash of high-end thefts that had been popping up nationwide. Local law enforcement agencies had been helpless to stop any of the crimes, and all of the thefts had been hidden from public knowledge. Lucas deVann had been placed in charge of the unit and had proven far more competent for either of their comfort. As far as the FBI was concerned, nobody needed to know that some of the most priceless works of art had been stolen, many of which had been replaced with highly detailed forgeries, so accurately crafted that there was still argument over their authenticity.

For six years, deVann and his men had studied Thomas and Michelle, or at least tried to. Only once had the stolen property been recovered, although much of it had turned up on the black market, mostly via anonymous online auctions. Twice, he and his men had managed to outbid the other auction entrants, but since the FBI had been unwilling to pay the amount promised at the first auction, none of the stolen items had been received.

Nor could any of the technical specialists that deVann had brought in back trace the auctions as they occurred. Despite all of their best efforts, they had been unable to trace from where the auctions were being held, unwilling to believe that the International Space Station was the hub for a major smuggling operation. There were too many safeguards in place, too many firewalls, and a higher security level than any of the federal agents had ever seen in place to prevent any traceability further beyond that. Not only had they been unable to trace the seller back to the source, but they had also been blocked from discovering the identities of the other bidders.

The second time the agents had won the auction, they had been authorized to deposit the funds as instructed in the hope that they could trace the funds to the perpetrators. Even the account information where they had been instructed to deposit the money had proved to be a dead end, as every penny was automatically transferred out of the account and the account was closed. The agents had been able to trace the funds through two leaps before they had lost track of it completely. Their last hope had been to track the package, once it was received, but that proved equally futile. It had arrived as a package return from their own office.

Now deVann was very definitely on their trail and Michelle could kick herself for pulling such a stupid maneuver. Despite her profession, being greedy was the most cardinal offense and the easiest method of being captured, and she had done precisely that. The freedom that she and Thomas had experienced with the inability of the FBI to trace their thefts had given her far more courage and audacity than warranted, and they were paying the price for her hubris. She had no idea how the task force had known that they would pull the museum job, but here he was, hauling their recent take away.

He would call it a victory, she knew.

He would be right.

Just because she had made a foolish mistake, that didn't mean that deVann shouldn't be praised and rewarded for capitalizing on it.

Michelle wasn't even really sure whether she was more upset about her blunder or the fact that the Phoenician artifacts were now out of reach to her. There had been some items in the crates that she didn't care very much about, things that she and Thomas had only taken because of their monetary value. But there were other things that she had wanted for her personal collection. Like the warrior statues that she had finally decided she wanted and the bird statue.

The money could be replaced, even though they would have to scramble a little more than Michelle found comfortable. Most of their resources had been expended and both of them had been counting on the profit from the upcoming auction. Bribery was expensive, after all, and so was research.

She growled and stomped down the hallway toward the living room, leaving Thomas to shut everything down and put it away, still angry with herself for the blunder. She would be angry with herself over that for some time yet, she was certain. Had she just driven directly to the supermarket and contacted Thomas from there, or even had she not stolen the van with the last crate to begin with, there would be no federal agents in her storage unit. The crates from that day's heist were not the only items in the storage unit, but at least she knew that none of the other items could be traced back to herself or Thomas, so perhaps all was not lost after all. They could rebuild; it wouldn't be the first time.

"It's not all gone," his voice cut into her brooding twenty minutes later. He sat down on the couch next to her and handed her a small package, wrapped in embossed white paper and topped with a silken pale blue bow.

She looked up at him in surprise. This was not one of the nationally celebrated holidays that she and Thomas participated in by rote. Neither of them had birthdays as recognized by the calendar they now followed, so there was no reasonable explanation for his sudden generosity.

"Take it," he urged her. "I had planned to give it to you later, but I think you should have it now."

Silently, she accepted the package. She ran a finger over the pretty bow before tugging one of the ends so that it fell across her lap. The paper was some that she had bought months ago, necessary to wrap gifts for a neighbor's baby shower. The embossed pattern of bunnies and ducks had been completely appropriate for its original use, but she had no need for such parties. "What is it?"

He chuckled without answering, so she did the only thing she could to discover an answer. Inside the box, nestled among mounds of crumpled tissue paper, a blind bronze bird slept.

SUITED FOR EXILE

Thomas and Michelle had spent the last twelve years moving from place to place. They never spent more than a year in any city before moving on and, for the most part, a year was longer than either of them liked. Where a year was their absolute limit, six months was better, four better yet. Spending great lengths of time in one area led to neighborly relationships that neither of them wanted or desired.

The same held true for countries of citizenship. For that, the time span could be longer. They had spent the last six years in the United States, with residencies in Europe and even South Africa before that. Now, it appeared as though it was about time for them to start thinking about leaving the United States. Michelle considered their options, debating on the risks and merits of the different countries to which they could relocate. Thomas was partial to Russia where his height wouldn't be quite as shocking, but Michelle wanted somewhere warmer. She had grown accustomed to short skirts and tall platform heels over the last few years and moving to a country of perpetual winter would diminish her ability to enjoy them.

"Just once," she explained, "I would like to go somewhere tropical."

Their address and citizenship weren't the only things they changed on a regular basis. Although they called themselves Thomas Ranger and Michelle Deva, those names were arbitrarily chosen the last time they moved and the names had suited their purposes well enough that neither of them minded. No matter where they lived on planet Earth, as long as they had something for other people to call them, that was all that was important.

Twelve years before, when they had crash landed on the small blue planet, they had no idea that they would be stuck there for so long, or that there would be so much variety even among the people of a singular planet. Sure, Earth had been one of their target destinations for exploration, but they had never intended to be stuck planet-side at all, let alone for so long. After the years they had spent on the planet, both had agreed that while it was a rich environment for taking what they wanted and selling to the highest bidder, there was very little of value off-planet. Valuable as some of the items may have been for the planetary residents, they wouldn't fetch very much money at all if sold elsewhere.

Damnable galactic constables anyway, she grumbled to herself. Had it not been for the critical damage their ship received in their last battle, they would have been long gone. Instead, they were stuck on this little backwater planet, the only planet in this system of a laughably small nine planets that could sustain anything that could be reasonably referred to as life.

They spent most of the first couple years of their exile trying to repair their damaged ship. However, they had discovered, to neither of their surprise, that the plasma cannons had done a remarkably thorough job of destroying their flight systems, navigation systems, and far too much of their shielding for the ship to be capable of leaving the atmosphere, let alone traveling the thousands of light years it would need to take to get them back into familiar territory. Without many of these systems up and running, they were forced to rely on the abysmal technology of the planet for their subsistence. Thankfully, the universal translators each of them had implanted worked despite the crash. Otherwise, even simple communication with the local population would have proven difficult.

They were lucky to have crashed onto a planet capable of sustaining life at all. Both of them realized this fact, although neither of them was anything close to being happy where they were. Not only was there life, there was life that they could resemble with only a minimal amount of camouflage. Had the locals resembled Verglings, or the blob-like creatures of Ralund, or even the gaseous forms that could be found on an assortment of planets, their efforts to blend in would have been futile. Five years of searching had only verified that no intergalactic freighters passed closely enough to the system they now resided within for them to be able to hail and barter for a ride elsewhere. They had been unable to locate any communication satellites within range to call back to their home system and request assistance, so they were truly and thoroughly stuck.

With no interstellar transports available, their next best option was to attempt to commission replacement parts for their ship, only to discover the futility of the idea. The planet's space program was so stunted that the inhabitants had barely been able to explore the planet's own moon, let alone any of the other planets or surrounding systems. What few space-travel supplies the population was capable of creating was far inferior to the levels that they would need to retrofit their own ship to leave. There was no escape.

Earth was nice enough, Michelle supposed, in its own way. The air was breathable; the food was edible, even if it was a little strange. There were so many native foods that the people calling themselves Thomas and Michelle made a concentrated effort to sample the cuisine of every culture they had been a part of, but both of them recognized that tasting everything would be a futile effort. Some of the foods they had discovered as they explored had been truly wonderful and even after leaving an area, they both took care to ensure they could still get some of it wherever they moved to. Others were so strange and disgusting that both of them were amazed the locals actually ate them without having been forced.

Breathable air and edible food were, at their core, basics for survival. Even if the needs of the body were met, there were thousands of other, smaller needs that most people took for granted. It had taken them time to discover that the needs of the average Earthling – humans, they called themselves, of course – were far reaching and complex.

For example, an astonishing number of the population was obsessed with artistic works of all varieties, at a level that the travelers had never seen before. Tangible art such as paintings, sculpture, and architectural designs were everywhere and non-tangible arts such as music and acting skill were high among the most revered arts on the planet. The sheer number of things available everywhere they looked, and the demand for these things, was almost overwhelming.

And, like everywhere, when people crave something enough to create it and charge exorbitant prices for it, there are always others willing to pay more, no matter how the object of their desire was acquired.

To Thomas and Michelle, that desire was a lifeline.

There were thousands, millions of cultures spread out across the planet and sprinkled throughout the history of the dominant race. Sure, they liked to refer to themselves as belonging to different races, but they were all humans beneath whatever cultural affectations they took upon themselves. They were all comprised of the same matter, in the same ratios, and although the coloring of their skin, hair, and eyes differed slightly from region to region, they all had the same basic anatomy. The really strange part, at least strange to Michelle and Thomas, was that not only did they appear similar to human cultures across the galaxy, many of the names they used were either the same or similar to names used elsewhere in the galaxy. That fact, if nothing else, made pronunciation much easier.

Each of these cultures had been determined to leave some tangible mark, some physical reminder that they had been. Some of these living memories were nothing more than broken pieces of clay and worn pieces of stone. Those items held little monetary value, although everyone held them in high regard for their undisputed historical value. Other cultures left fantastic sculptures, bronze, brass, silver, and gold wrought works, and treasures of every variety. Some were vast, with pieces being found constantly, where others were limited, with only a handful of relics left to show that someone, some culture, had once existed.

These artistic pieces had swiftly garnered the attention of the space travelers. They had arrived with no prospects, no way to maintain themselves, and no currency of the planet. They had needed to find a way to supplement themselves, and they had found it.

Even better, the ability to acquire and resell items of high value, whether it was smuggled platinum from the mines on Ralund or hijacked freighters of Myrite from the Oberron system, happened to be a specialty of theirs. They had made a name for themselves as dealers in all things stolen many years before and it was those actions, or rather the escape therefrom, that had caused their exile to Earth in the first place.

The Queen of Diamonds and the Knave of Spades, as they were known throughout the galaxy, had once been the leaders of a force to be reckoned with. Their actions on Earth, as impressive and frustrating as they may have been to deVann and the other authorities responsible for investigating them, were nothing compared to the heists that they were known for on other planets. Out in other systems and in charge of their Deck, as they referred to their troupe, they were experts in bypassing security systems of the highest levels. National treasuries, military equipment, and experimental technologies had been within their grasp. Billions of credits, the primary currency used for trade throughout the galaxy, passed through their accounts every year, unfettered by silly things like laws.

On Earth, however, the best they could hope for was to keep their skills, if not challenged, at least in practice on the abysmally low technology world. Some of the places they had looked at for residence had been more technologically advanced than others while some had been in possession of almost nothing of technological value.

Up to this point, they had been easily able to outwit the local authorities, even deVann and his team of specialists, without relying on much of their technological expertise. Neither of them had seen the need.

Now, it appeared that their shopping habits were starting to catch up to them.

Another warning interrupted her reverie and she leapt to her feet to see what had happened. Knave met her at the hidden console, where he already had the panel open and activated.

"What's going on?" she asked as she stepped up to look around him.

"Seattle," he answered without looking down at her. Not that the answer told her anything more than what was plainly visible on the monitor. She recognized the interior of the house that she and Knave had moved out of only three months before. There were federal agents flooding the house, led by deVann.

Diamond stared at the screen, dumbfounded. "How did they find that place?" she asked. "We were nowhere near there!"

"I have no idea."

Maybe they had blundered worse than they had imagined, Diamond thought. She had believed that the theft of the transport van had led the FBI to their storage facility, but they hadn't gone anywhere near their Seattle house in months – since moving out, in fact.

"What is going on?"

She wasn't worried about what the agents would find inside. Although the house appeared to be filled with priceless artifacts, most of the art and décor was fake, replicas that the pair of them had created. No, what worried her was the implication of having FBI agents in a place where there was no reason for them to be.

Her suspicions had been right. The task force was much closer to finding them than either of them had recognized.

KNOW YOUR ENEMY

The pair of rogues held themselves in high alert, waiting for any signal that would indicate that their location had been compromised. With the appearance of the FBI at their storage unit and their house in Seattle, neither of them was certain any longer that their current residence was still unknown. Knave stood for hours before his bank of monitors, waiting for any of their other alarms to sound and cycling through the video feeds from hundreds of cameras, just to be sure that their alarm systems hadn't been tampered with.

Diamond, keeping up the pretense that she had been rendered unconscious just as the driver of the van she stole had been, waited until the approximate time where the driver would be waking up from the electric charge she had given him before heading out to call the police and report her own assault. It wouldn't do for the driver to remember he had a passenger and lead the authorities to wonder what had happened to her.

The police, reacting slowly as many metropolitan police departments are wont to do, kept her waiting for over half an hour between when she placed the call and when the first patrol cruiser arrived. By that time, she had made her way to a local coffee-house and ordered herself a drink. Although she shared Knave's dislike of coffee, she had discovered that with enough sweeteners and flavorings, the coffee itself was hardly noticeable.

Coffee was a large part of the culture in this area, similar to what it had been when they had lived in Seattle. It seemed like every other corner in town had a coffee shop or kiosk waiting to give the locals their daily fix. The first time they had discovered this phenomenon, both of them had sampled hundreds of different varieties of the beverage, both discovering that there was really no way to make it enjoyable. Worse, it had given Knave tremendous heartburn, so he refused to drink any more of the acrid beverage. While Diamond didn't enjoy the coffees any more than did her friend, she didn't have as physical a reaction as he did to it and so was able to consume it on occasion, but only when the situation truly warranted it. Now, she felt, was one of those times.

As she had anticipated, the police officers, named Jenkins and Singer, took Diamond not to the police station, but to the federal building. With deVann and his men already on their heels, Diamond had figured that there was a high probability that the task force would be far more interested in getting her statement than the already-overworked local police.

She was escorted into the building and taken to the third floor, where another pair of armed escorts dismissed Jenkins and Singer. Wick and Fisher, two agents that Diamond recognized on sight as being a part of deVann's crew, were friendly but wary. She knew that both of them were honest and respectable, at least as honest and respectable as a federal agent could be, and she knew that she would have to tread quietly while they were near. Worse than being honest, these men were smart.

"Why am I here?" she asked in a timid voice, trying to look even smaller than she already was. For just this purpose, she had foregone her traditional platform heels. Now, at barely over a unit and a half tall, both of the agents towered over her and she made sure they knew it.

Defenseless women. Men on this planet had been trained from birth to believe that there was nothing more helpless, nothing more in need of their compassion, than a woman who appeared to be completely at their mercy. Of course, there were always exceptions, but on the whole that had been her experience.

Fisher looked down at her, meeting her enormous, watery green eyes with his own stoic blue ones. As she let the fear become more obvious in her face, her body language and posturing, a small twitch appeared in Fisher's cheek, and she knew that he had fallen into her trap as easily as she had prepared it. He saw her as a victim already, nothing more than what she let him see. All she had to do was not overact, lest they suspect she was lying to them.

Wick was a little less trusting than his partner. "We think you might have evidence in an ongoing case," he explained with barely a glance at her. "More than that, we're not at liberty to discuss at this point."

When they arrived at the end of the hallway, Fisher knocked twice on the door and opened it, gesturing for her to enter first. She shot him a frightened smile before ducking beneath his arm – a barely-needed maneuver, but one that would solidify his impression of her smallness and helplessness - and walked into deVann's office.

She had seen the room before, of course. She and Knave made a point of knowing their opposition as well as possible, so both of them had spent much time in this office, perusing his files and spying on his computer activity. If the agency had any idea of how easy it was to break in by posing as a member of the local cleaning service they used, she was sure that he would have secured his office, and particularly all of the information inside it, much more thoroughly. Not that it would have mattered, of course. What passed for a secure computer system on this planet was child's play in comparison to those she had been trained to bypass.

"Have a seat," deVann's voice cut into her thoughts as she stepped across the room toward him. "Miss Deva, isn't it?" He pronounced it DEE-vah, as most people did upon meeting her.

deVann was taller than she had realized, closer to two units than the unit and eight tenths she had expected when he stood to greet her. His eyes were a deep, warm brown, and the shadow across his chin told her that he needed to shave more than once a day to keep his skin clear. He wore his usual black suit and tie with only the slightest bulge at his hip to show that he was armed.

She nodded, for all appearances too frightened to speak as she sat onto one of the hard metal folding chairs that waited in front of his desk. "It's…" she took a deep breath. "It's Deva." She pronounced it the way she liked it better, DAY-vah. Not that it mattered, of course, but she had noticed how picky some Earthlings were about the pronunciation of their names and had picked the affectation as one of her own quirks.

For this name, at least. Once she changed her identity again, which was likely to be very soon, she wouldn't care how anyone pronounced it.

"Sorry, Miss Deva." He said it correctly that time. "I understand you were involved in an assault this morning." His tone was calm, gentle, but she could see the steely resolve in his eyes. He wasn't about to be fooled by her act, so as soon as Fisher and Wick closed the door behind her without entering themselves, she took another deep breath and worked to compose herself.

"Can you tell me what happened?"

"I'm not really sure," she answered after a brief pause. "I remember we were driving to the airport, but the next thing I knew, I woke up on a bench in the park."

"Do you know if anything unusual happened on the drive?" he asked. "As I understand, you were transporting some items of value."

Even as he spoke, Diamond wondered if she had made another mistake. Had he discovered that she had been involved in the heist after all? She hadn't left any evidence in the storage unit, she was certain, but had something in her actions given her away?

No, she reassured herself, refusing to let her doubts guide her actions. She had done everything correctly, and the only thing Agent deVann knew was that she was a witness. There was no reason to start having doubts now, and if she dropped her guard, she was certain that deVann would pounce on the opening.

"We were transporting items from the Egyptian exhibit," she explained. "There was a fire at the museum, so all of the artifacts were being transported to the airport for safety."

"Was the airport aware that these items were coming?"

She nodded, a short dip of the head. "They had been preparing to accept them later in the week, but I'm sure someone called them when the fire started to let them know we were delivering them early."

deVann made a note on the yellow pad before him on his desk. "Do you know who called the airport?"

"No," she shook her head, honestly bewildered, not a position she found comfortable. Why was he asking about that? "It was probably Danielle O'Connor. I think she usually takes care of that." Danielle was the security supervisor at the museum, and Diamond's guess wasn't just a guess.

Diamond herself hadn't had anything to do with the crates once they left the museum. Except, of course, for the crates she had stolen. "All I know is that we needed to get the packages out of the building before they were destroyed."

After filling his page with notes, deVann flipped to a fresh page and continued to write. "Were there any unusual people hanging around while the packages were being loaded?" he asked as he looked back up at her. "Or while they were being packed?"

"I..." her voice trailed off as she tried to think. "I don't remember seeing anyone unusual, but there were so many people, and everyone was running around, I doubt I would have noticed if a whole tour group came through." She smiled at him in chagrin. "It was pretty hectic."

"Understandable." He made a couple more notes, and Diamond wondered whether he was really getting as much out of their conversation as he seemed to, or if it was just a small intimidation tactic. "You left with the last van, is that correct?"

"Yes. As soon as we loaded the last of the artifacts, I got into the van and we drove to the airport."

"What made you do that?"

"What?" She blinked at him again, not quite sure what he was asking.

"What made you leave with the van instead of getting into your own car and driving away? That's what most of the other people did."

"I didn't have a car there," she explained. "I take the bus to work. Once the last of the crates got loaded, it was time to start worrying about getting myself out of the way."

He nodded again and made a small sound of thoughtfulness as he jotted down more notes. "You're a volunteer at the museum, aren't you? Not a full-time employee?"

"No, I'm a volunteer."

"But most of the other volunteers took off as soon as the fire alarms went off. Why did you stay behind to help with the loading?"

"Because it needed to be done," she answered slowly. "Those artifacts are some of the most amazing pieces of Egyptian history, and the thought of them being destroyed..." she shuddered at the very idea.

"You're saying that you stayed behind, despite the fire, for the artifacts?" he raised an eyebrow at her in doubt at her assertion. "Why were they so important?"

She sighed, but she already had the answer. In fact, none of the questions he had asked so far had been outside the range of what she had prepared for with the exception of the questions about who had called the airport. "I started volunteering at the museum because they have all of these great exhibits, all of these amazing things that most people could never see unless they were on display. Each piece that's brought into the building, no matter how small it is or how long or short of a time it stays there, is a piece of our history, a piece of who we are.

"The Egyptian exhibit is no different, but on the other hand, it's even more. So many of the artifacts that were once in the tombs, in the pyramids, have been stolen, that there aren't very many left. So yeah," she looked up to meet his eyes again. "I think they're that important."

He evaluated her for a long moment before changing the direction of his questions. "What about the driver? Was he a person you were familiar with?"

"Not especially, no. He had been a driver for us a few times before, but then, we use Christopherson a lot."

"Was he acting suspiciously that day? Or doing anything out of the ordinary?"

She laughed. "I wouldn't know. This was the first time I'd ever hitched a ride with any of them."

"Could you tell if you were being followed?"

She shook her head again. "I wasn't really looking," she admitted ruefully. "I looked back at the museum a couple of times just out of curiosity about where the fire was, but I wasn't paying a lot of attention to the other people on the road."

deVann wrote down a few more notes and flipped the page. "What about when you were attacked? What can you remember about that?"

"Nothing." When he looked at her with an eyebrow raised, she shrugged. "We were driving, and then I woke up." She thought for a moment before continuing. "But I think we stopped, though. Maybe at a red light."

"Do you remember anyone else entering the vehicle?"

She shook her head thoughtfully. "No. It was just me and him." She stopped suddenly and looked up at him in surprise. "What happened to the artifacts?" Her voice rose in alarm. "Were they stolen?"

"They were recovered," he reassured her. "We're still checking to make sure everything's there, but it looks like the people trying to rob you didn't manage to take any of it."

She let out a sigh of relief, although she was fuming inside. She and Knave had stolen those crates fairly and, though she wanted them back, she knew that she wasn't likely to get another opportunity like the one they had just lost.

After only a few more questions, deVann called Wick back into his office and had him give Diamond a ride home. "Thank you for your help, Ms. Deva," he handed her an official-looking business card as she was escorted out the door. "If you can remember anything else, please give me a call."

A BASKET OF FRUIT

As soon as she walked into the house, Diamond stormed to the back hallway, where Knave had pulled up a trio of stools from the kitchen. He sat on one of them, leaning back against the opposite wall as he watched for any change in the monitors. The other stool worked as an erstwhile table as it held a cup of tea and a half-eaten roast beef sandwich.

"Any change?" she asked him as she picked up his tea to have a drink and surveyed the monitors. "Ugh," she groaned as she set the tea back down. "What is that?"

"Oolong," he responded without looking away from the holo map. "I think it's from China."

"Well, it's disgusting," she retorted as she headed to the kitchen to fix herself a cup of lemon mint.

"No change," Knave's voice startled her by its proximity and Diamond almost missed her cup as she added a dollop of honey to sweeten her beverage.

She sighed. "At least that was all they found." The house and storage unit had been a blow to both of them, but it was far from the roust that they had feared. Although it had initially seemed as though the federal agents would find every last scrap of their activities, their raids had stopped in Seattle. There were other houses and other storage areas, and more could be procured if it became necessary.

Without much to do, she wandered out to the living room. "The agents seemed to believe that there was someone watching the exhibit as it was being loaded," she informed Knave as she flipped on the television. "They hinted that we were followed from the museum..." Her voice trailed off as an image of the house the FBI had overtaken appeared on the screen, a reasonably attractive woman standing in the foreground.

"...of this drug manufacturing facility." The reporter was already mid-story, but Diamond didn't need to know anything more than the half sentence she had just heard to understand what the FBI had released to the press about the raid.

She had to resist the urge to smash her teacup against the wall and Knave, sensing her wrath, gently released the porcelain cup from her clenched fingertips. "Don't blame them," he said gently as he placed the cup out of her immediate reach. "They're just working with the reports they got."

"Oh, I know that." Emerald fire burned in her eyes as she clenched and unclenched her fists. "Of all the things they could have said, did they really have to go with a *drug house*?"

For all their faults, Knave and Diamond had decided within months of landing on the planet that the drug trade, although lucrative, was one arena where they would never involve themselves. They both understood that there was money to be had in the manufacture and sale of chemical contraband, a *lot* of money, but it didn't take long to discover exactly how dangerous those substances were. The people of Earth had enough problems; the alien pair didn't understand their apparent need to make their lives even worse.

Even worse than the presence of the drugs was that those who used them behaved in terribly erratic fashion and even occasionally died as a result from their intoxication. They had quickly discovered by a basic perusal of the news agencies that there were a handful of chemicals readily for sale that caused those who used them to become violent and dangerous. While Diamond and Knave could respect violent and dangerous people, they abhorred anything that caused people to become completely irrational.

Not that they avoided the drug trade completely. There had been plenty of times where one or the other of them had been out and about in town and had been approached by an innocuous-looking street peddler. At first, they had been satisfied with removing the peddlers from damaging the local population, but they knew that these hawkers were not acting alone.

Diamond and Knave knew, probably better than anyone else on the planet, that the only way to stop them was to go to the top. The foot soldiers selling the contraband on the streets were nothing in comparison to those who ran the show.

They had begun a campaign of eradication, using all of the tricks that they relied on for other, equally dishonorable, pursuits. As a result, the entire continental western seaboard, from Seattle to San Diego, was more drug-free than at any time in the last thirty years, according to the last statistics Diamond had uncovered. Areas further inland had started to see a change in the availability of contraband as a result as well.

The reason for the reduction was simple: there was nothing left. Knave and Diamond had eliminated every supplier, ever manufacturer, and every large-scale importer that they had come across, and the peddlers had soon learned that although the addicts would pay top dollar for their goods, the odds of cocaine, heroin, and methamphetamines making it to market, among other illicit chemicals, was slight.

This focused eradication was why Diamond had reacted so strongly to the slanderous reports on the news. The FBI had no way of knowing that the thieves they had been searching for were the same people who had minimized the drug traffic in their beloved city, but it galled her nonetheless.

This assault on their character would have to be responded to.

She absently reached for the phone that waited on the small table next to the couch and, without looking, hit the button that would connect her to one of her favorite contacts.

"Yes, I'd like to order a delivery, please," she stated politely but emotionlessly as soon as someone picked up on the other end. "No, I have a special order."

She explained exactly what she wanted to have delivered and, thanks to her earlier meeting at the FBI's headquarters, she knew just which suite to have it sent to. She already knew the suite, of course, due to her previous surveillance of the office, but now she was certain that the targeted recipient would be available. She paid for the order with a credit card that had never existed and hung up the phone.

"Was that really necessary?" Knave handed her back her cup of tea, which was now cool enough to drink without scalding her tongue.

"Oh yeah," she responded, her voice almost a growl as she sniffed at her cup. "If that doesn't give them the message, I'm not sure what will."

One of the more unusual calling cards of the Queen of Diamonds and Knave of Spades had always been one of her personal favorites. Among all of the traditions they had begun since the beginning of their felonious relationship, the sending of gift baskets had been the one to garner them the most fame and notoriety. These baskets were generally floral or fruit-based in nature, with each of their playing cards and other assorted but relevant items included as needed. Each basket was personalized for the recipient and the intended message, generated as obviously as possible in the contained items.

Edible Arrangements was a small company that was based in Portland, which Diamond had discovered long before moving into the area. The company specialized in decorative but delicious fruit arrangements that looked more like decadent bouquets than fruit salads. Among the strawberries and melons in the arrangement she had ordered for delivery to the task force, Diamond also requested that a pair of playing cards be added, as well as a "Drug-Free America" advertising pamphlet and a keychain advertising the Seattle Seahawks, one of the most famous sports teams to be found in the Seattle area.

As usual, as long as their contact at Edible Arrangements was paid extra for the inconvenience of having to gather the requested items, a service not usually offered, they accepted the order at face value and promised delivery by noon of the next day.

Less than a minute after Diamond hung up the phone, it rang again. Because he was still standing behind the couch and was closer to it than Diamond was, Knave answered it.

His expression faded from the slightly amused smile that he had worn in reaction to Diamond's angst, turning instead to fierce concentration. When Diamond tried to inquire what had changed, he held up a hand to silence her.

Not liking to be shushed, even less liking to be outside of the conversation, Diamond scowled and settled back down to wait. Her patience was surely being tested this day. She tried to stay as quiet as possible, hoping in vain to hear what was being said on the other end of the line. Although she could hear some noise, she was unable to make out any words.

On the other hand, Knave's scowl broke as he listened to whoever was on the other end of the line and a wide grin spread across his face. "Thank you," he said at long last, the first words he had uttered since his greeting upon answering. "I'll get that deposited into your account within the hour."

Diamond, her cup forgotten on the ill-named coffee table, turned around in her seat so that she was kneeling against the back of the couch and all but quivering in anticipation by the time Knave broke the connection.

"What is it?" The question spilled out before Knave had a chance to pace the handset back into its charging base. "What's happened?"

"Do you remember Sherman?" He asked her, his eyes alight with excitement.

"Sherman?" She had to think about it. The name sounded familiar, but she was slow in placing a face to go with the name. "Isn't he that idiot that thinks the whole world is run by robots and that they've poisoned the cows to keep the humans in line?"

"Yep, that's the one."

To call Sherman a conspiracy buff was like calling a Grand Prix racer a moderately skilled driver. The last time that Knave and Diamond had been forced to deal with Sherman in person, he had spent the better part of an hour telling her about the radioactive fish that the government-robots put into each can of tuna so that they could monitor where every person on the planet was at any given time. When Diamond had questioned him about how the government managed to track the people who hadn't eaten the tainted fish, he hadn't had much of an explanation. At least, not one that made any sense at all.

"What now?" She couldn't hide the tone of exasperation. The last thing she needed was to have that blowhard try and drag them into another of his stupid ideas to lead the people out from under their overlords. "And why did you promise him money?"

"Because he might have found something this time." When she looked up at him with one eyebrow raised in doubt, he continued. "He just had to warn me that the invasion's begun."

"What invasion?" she sighed. "Is it the squirrels with mad cow disease again? The African honeybees that everyone is supposed to be lethally allergic to? Or the cockroaches with cameras attached to their bodies?" She could have gone on further, but the fact that his smile hadn't wavered made her stop.

"Aliens?" she whispered, barely able to contain the hope from shining through.

Knave nodded. "Apparently, a space craft landed in Southern Oregon last week. He's been tracking it, but it hasn't moved since landing."

"Hasn't moved?" She looked at him, one sculpted eyebrow raised. "Does that mean it crashed? Or does that mean it's not a spaceship at all?" As excited as she was about the prospect of finding another ship to get them off the planet, she didn't want to get her hopes up too far, only to discover that it was some sort of remote-controlled toy. They had both seen enough videos on the internet to know how easy it was to make it appear that aliens had arrived. For the first year or so after their arrival, she and Knave had been fooled by more than one of the realistic images, only to be sorely disappointed upon discovering the truth.

"Who knows?" He grinned at her. "And who cares." He tapped at the keyboard of a nearby computer, transferring the promised funds into Sherman's account. "Either its nothing and we spend a few days on a wild goose chase, or it's *not* nothing, and we have a way off this forsaken rock."

Her breath caught in her throat as his words sank in. Twelve years. For twelve years, she had hoped to find some way for the pair of them to escape back to the stars, back to the home where they belonged, that even the idea that their escape *might* be near was heartbreaking.

They might have a way to get out of there after all.

This was a good thing, she realized, considering how close the FBI was getting to catching them.

THE SHIMMER IN THE DESERT

They didn't waste any time heading down to southern Oregon to check on the validity of Sherman's information. While Diamond packed some basic necessities for the trip, Knave called the pilot of their private Gulfstream jet to ready the plane.

As usual, Michaels was unfazed by the sudden travel plans. "Will you be traveling alone?" he inquired, "or should I prepare for more passengers?"

"No," Knave reassured him. "This will be just the two of us."

"Very well, sir." Michaels's English heritage was somehow more apparent over the telephone than it was in person. Knave suspected that, though Michaels was definitely not a native of the United States, his accent was deliberately exaggerated. He could definitely appreciate his dedication to character, regardless of the validity of his accent.

"Two hours," Knave said as he hung up the phone. "That should be plenty of time for everything to be ready."

"More than enough for me," Diamond answered as she zipped her suitcase closed. "I'm ready to go now."

It didn't take long for Knave to ensure that all of his requirements would be met as well and both of them tried to keep the tone light as they determined which things to take with them and which to leave behind. Although neither of them had stated the thought openly, it was understood that there were equal chances of this being a one-way trip, with them never seeing their home in the Pacific Northwest again and being a colossal waste of time.

However, even knowing that the odds of finding a ship that was both locatable and flight-capable were not in their favor, neither of them could help the thrill of anticipation and the warm spreading of an emotion that neither of them had felt for most of the twelve years they had been stuck on Earth.

Hope.

One entire suitcase was filled with an assortment of the items she and Knave had stolen over the years. A small painting by one of the artists known as a Master was rolled into a sleeve and tucked along an edge. The blind bird nestled next to it, securely wrapped in paper. A wooden box containing an assortment of royal regalia went in next. The royal jewels were from no earthly kingdom, they were the last items she had stolen before being stranded on Earth. It had been the constables from that planet who had shot them down in an attempt to abort the theft.

For his part, Knave had a similar, although smaller, bag of items stolen from the planet. His items were more perfunctory in nature, memorabilia of some of the places he had raided rather than items they had targeted. He had security badges, name plates, even a desk calendar from one famous legislator who had irritated him many years ago.

Michaels met them at the small airstrip and personally loaded their bags onto the plane. He was a stout older man, closer to fifty than to forty, but the vigor of his youth hadn't left him yet. As usual, he wore dun-colored khakis and a white button-down shirt that was rolled up to the elbows. His vibrant blue eyes glittered with humor as he moved the suitcases and other bags. "Travelling lightly, I see."

The Gulfstream waited on the tarmac, dull grey-white with royal blue and sunshine yellow markings of identification. This was the latest version of the expensive line of planes and Knave and Diamond knew that there were only a handful of Gulfstream Sevens, commonly shortened to G7, in the United States. It wasn't an expense that they would have spent on their own, being more than willing to settle for a G5 or even a G4, but it had been part of a trade agreement during one of their latest auctions and both of them had fallen in love with the sleek aircraft as soon as they saw it.

Sure, it wasn't a space-worthy battleship, but it was better by far than flying commercial. Upon their acceptance of the plane, Diamond had commented that she would have gladly traded every item in that auction to never have to wait in line to be frisked at an airliner's security checkpoint ever again. Michaels had come with the plane, as had a flight attendant that Knave had fired almost immediately for bringing a date aboard for a rendezvous. While they could appreciate the audacity, neither of them appreciated the breach in security.

The journey itself was uneventful. Once they were settled into the soft leather seats, they poured themselves flutes of chilled champagne as the plane taxied down the runway. They toasted to possibilities, both of them fervently hoping that there would be more than smoke, mirrors, and conspiracy theories to find when they landed.

True to his word, Michaels had arranged for transportation once they arrived. A large, tough-looking Lincoln Navigator waited nearby, and the keys were handed over while their luggage was deposited into the SUV's spacious back.

"So," Diamond broke the silence once they had put almost a mile behind them, "do you think there's really something there?"

"Doubtful," Knave answered with hardly any hesitation. "If something had landed, there would have been news of it all over the place. FBI, CIA, even Homeland Security would be running all over the place, trying to figure out how much of a threat it is." And he would have known about it by now as well, she knew. Knave had immediately scanned all of the federal communications, searching for some sign that they had spotted Sherman's aliens.

Her hope flagged at his statement, although she realized his words were true. Their own landing had caused quite a stir and it had been months before they had been able to return to the crash site unmolested.

Not that the authorities had found anything while they were searching, of course. One of the few systems that hadn't been damaged in either the attack or the landing was the cloaking system that bent rays of light around the craft, effectively rendering it invisible.

"Do you know where you're going?" she asked as he turned off the main road and onto a small, little-used road that could more accurately be called a path than anything else.

"According to Sherman," he answered, gritting his teeth as the truck bounced over a series of deep potholes, "the ship crashed a few miles, about five thousand units, this way. I figure the sooner we get off the main road, the better chance we'll have of figuring out where we're supposed to be."

That made sense. There were hundreds of cars, trucks, and motorcycles travelling along the highway, so if there was a ship to be seen, it would have been noticed if it was visible from the highway. "But couldn't we have gotten something with suspension?" she demanded as she was thrown against the passenger door.

"Wasn't my call," he said, clutching the wheel but not letting off the gas. "Apparently when I said I wanted a truck, Michaels thought this was what I meant."

They argued for another mile until Knave, to Diamond's great relief, stopped the truck. They were at the edge of an empty field, farmland of some variety, with a small herd of cows grazing at the far end.

They hopped out of the truck, scanning the area for any signs that a ship had crashed, but there was nothing to be found. None of the nearby trees showed broken branches or other damage that would indicate the presence of a craft, and there were no troughs in the ground, either.

They walked along the side of the field, first in one direction and then another, hope fading with every step they took. When they arrived at the Navigator with nothing to show for an afternoon of searching, Diamond could have screamed in frustration.

Not that she was surprised, she reasoned to herself. This wasn't the first time that she and Knave had been called to action over a supposed alien landing, as their visit to New Mexico had painfully demonstrated. As much as the residents of this planet refused to admit that there were other forms of life in the galaxy, they sure spent a lot of time discussing whether such life had been found.

"What is that?" Diamond stopped, her hand on the door handle and ready to climb into the passenger seat, when Knave spoke.

"What?"

He was looking out into the field, one hand raised to shield his eyes from the fading sunlight. "Something's shimmering out there."

"What do you mean, shimmering?" She raised a shading hand as well, trying to see what he saw.

"There it is again." Leaving the door open, he jogged out into the field, heading in the same direction he had been looking.

Diamond sighed and followed. This had happened before as well, both of them so eager to find something that their eyes, their ears, all of their senses began to play tricks on them.

Apparently Knave's hopes had been raised even further than hers had. "There's nothing there!" she called after him.

He stopped, lowering his hand and slowly stepping to the side, looking between her and the nothing that was before him. Slowly, an expression of pure glee spread across his features. "It's here."

Diamond could hardly believe what she was hearing. She could see that there was nothing before them, but he sounded so certain, so positive, that she had to wonder.

She stepped up next to him, squinting at the light. "I don't see it."

"You have to look sideways," he explained as he turned to face her. "Look at me."

She turned to face him, and out of the corner of her eye, she could see something shimmering, only yards away from where she stood. She gasped and turned to face it, but the apparition faded.

"It's got to be a new cloaking system," Knave explained as he turned back to their waiting truck to get his supplies.

"And it doesn't look like it crashed. I think it landed here."

A lightly-colored aerosol spray, one of Diamond's own inventions, allowed them a better view of the ship. Although they couldn't see it precisely, the spray was much too fine and the ship too large, they were able to get basic estimates of its dimensions. Those Diamond plugged into her laptop computer to generate a wire-frame diagram and get a better idea of what they were looking at.

"It's an Albatross," she breathed in awe once she recognized the design. Albatrosses were some of the fastest ships that had been in service when they had disappeared from the space game, for one to appear for their use now seemed too good to be true.

Which it probably was. Because Albatross-class ships were so fast, and able to travel long distances without needing to refuel, they were frequently used as scout ships – which meant that a scout team was likely nearby.

"We have to hurry."

Knave, recognizing the danger as swiftly as she had, was already pulling more tools out of his pack. "Entry port's near the front of the middle section," he said, more to himself than to Diamond, as though trying to remind himself that he knew how and where to break in. "It's ahead of the wings."

He was correct, so Diamond didn't bother to say anything in return. What he needed now was to restore his confidence, to remember that he was every bit as good today as he had been twelve years ago. She left him alone.

Knave pulled a set of magnetic climbing poles, specifically designed years before and one of the few items they had found a use for after landing on Earth, for climbing sheer – or almost sheer - metal walls. He snapped one into place just above his own eye level, and another just above that. Using the higher one to lift his body weight, he lifted himself until he was standing in mid-air and placed a third pole.

When Knave was high enough, Diamond began to climb up as well. Although she didn't have the upper body strength that Knave possessed, she was light and limber, so jumping to reach a higher pole was easier for her to do than him.

They maneuvered, him placing poles and her gathering them up as they passed, until they were directly over the section where the entrance port would be located. There, Diamond placed a pair of poles evenly but further apart and braced herself for balance as Knave unwound a thin coil of rope.

She stabilized him, holding most of his weight as he slipped down toward the ground, now more than two stories below, so that he could reach the access panel.

"It's a multi-key touchpad," he called up to her, relief evident in his voice. "I should be able to get through this no problem."

"Good," she called back down to him, her voice showing no sign of the strain her body was under. "Because I think you've gained a few pounds."

There was nothing inside the ship to explain who the owners had been, or to explain what its purpose on Earth was. There were, of course, tracking systems in place, specifically designed to let whoever was in charge of monitoring the ship's progress know where they were and if they were in trouble.

"If we remove that now," Knave explained when Diamond pointed out the monitors to him, "it'll let them know the ship's been taken."

"I know that," she snapped back at him. "I was just letting *you* know where it was so when we're ready to leave, we can disable it."

"Right," he said with chagrin. "It's just been a while and if we blow this, we're really in trouble."

"I know," she said much more softly in a reassuring tone. "But we know what we're doing; we've done this hundreds of times." She decided that the conversation would be better served by changing the subject. "Do you have the overrides done?"

"Working on it," he grunted from beneath a console. They had to change all of the security codes and passwords, not specifically to gain control of the ship, which they could do at any point, but in case the original owners returned. It simply wouldn't do for the owners to return while they were still halfway through stealing the ship. Knave had started by overriding the entry codes and was proceeding system by system, changing all of the codes so that they would have complete, immediate control as soon as they took off, rather than the absolute basic amount of control they would have if they hadn't waited.

The last time they had needed to go through the procedure to recode an entire ship had been more than fifteen years ago. Back then, it had taken the pair a matter of minutes to race through all

of the systems. While they confirmed that they had not forgotten the process in the interim, their substantially reduced speed
showed just how far out of practice they had gotten while stuck
on the blue ball.

"On the positive side," she commented, her voice cheerful,
"whoever we're leaving behind won't be stuck here like we were."

"Good for them," he grunted in response. "Why do you think
that?"

"Because whoever's got the money to send out a ship like this
one," she thumped the console above his head, causing him to
let out a string of colorful expletives, "can afford to send out a
retrieval team for them."

"Unless it's IG."

She thought about it for a moment before answering. "It's not."

"Why do you think that?"

"Because even if the stealth system's new, this ship is at least
fifteen years old. The IG always uses brand-new ships. None of
them would be caught dead using a recycled old hag like this
one."

The Interplanetary Government, the organization that over-
sees almost all of the inhabited planets in the galaxy that were
capable of interplanetary travel, didn't know the meaning of the
term frugal. Whether it was ships to send into war zones, soldiers
to die on the battlefront, or simply ensuring that the public image
they held was one of grandeur, her assessment had been correct.
There was no way this was an IG ship.

"Besides," she added, "the markings are all wrong."

"But do you recognize them?"

She thought in silence for a long moment before shaking her
head, even though there was no way for him to see the gesture. "I
don't think I've seen them before."

"They're Vergling."

"No, they aren't." The Verglings were a race of small, highly territorial people who controlled most of the Oberron system. They had declined to join the IG, citing excessive security fees and trade restrictions. So far, or at least as far as Diamond knew, they were holding firm on that decision. "This is their language, but it's not part of their fleet."

"Nope," he agreed as he slid back out from under the console. "It's a scout, just like you thought. But I don't think there are any Verglings on planet."

She had to laugh at his assessment, even though she agreed with it. She and Knave were able to blend in with the Earthlings, but that was only because each of their particular species was similar enough to being human that the locals overlooked the differences. Verglings, on the other hand, were insectoid and less than half the size of a human. The closest thing that Earth had to a Vergling would be an ant, but ants didn't grow nearly large enough for them to blend in successfully.

"Well, if it's not Verglings, then who do you think it is?" she asked once she stopped laughing.

"No clue. But that should do it."

"Already?" her eyebrows shot up in surprise. She had expected the system overrides to take much longer, but it had barely been more than fifteen minutes.

"It's not all of it," he said, accurately reading her expression, "but it's enough for us to have control without having to scramble once we're in the air."

That made sense. Completely overriding the ship would probably take days, if not longer. As long as the basic command codes were theirs, it would be good enough. She pulled out her phone.

"Hi, Michaels," she said when his voice came on the line. "I have good news for you."

"Do you?" She couldn't tell from his voice whether he was amused at the call or simply being polite, but it didn't matter anymore.

"Congratulations," she continued. "You are now the proud owner of one Gulfstream Seven, slightly used."

As he made sounds of confusion and surprise, she continued. "I trust that you will take good care of it. Of course, this means that your services will no longer be needed."

She hung up before he could protest further and grinned at her companion. "So," she said. "Are you ready to go?"

"Absolutely," he said as he settled into the captain's seat. She sat at the front control panel and began to flip switches and press buttons, and she could hear him doing the same behind her.

"Let's go home."

FAMILIAR TERRITORY

As with all planetary systems, Earth was a part of a larger solar system. Although the Earthlings hadn't named their sun, they had named most of their planets but not the system itself. As they flew through the solar system, past small rocky dwarfs and larger gas giants, Diamond felt a sense of relief mixed with trepidation.

Relief because they were finally able to leave the planet's surface and rejoin the space-faring universe they belonged to.

The trepidation stemmed from the long road they knew they had ahead of them. According to IG law, which was the standard most planetary governments followed, even if they weren't a part of it, a person was presumed to be dead after five years, so long as there has been no communication from them and it could not be determined where they were. It had been more than twice that length since Knave and Diamond had spoken to anyone, and she wasn't sure how their return would be received.

They would have to move completely out of the system before activating the spatial compression drive. That particular type of

engine, which had quickly become standard on long-range vehicles, compressed the space ahead of the vehicle and expanded
the space behind it so that the vehicle actually travelled a much
shorter distance than the actual distance between starting point
and destination. That expansion and contraction, however, caused
massive gravitational fluctuations that could damage planetary
bodies, such as planets and moons, or even disrupt their orbits
if activated within too close of a proximity, so each vehicle that
had a spatial compression drive installed also came with some
heavy safety protocols in the activation software to prevent such
damage.

According to the onboard computers, it would take at least
six hours of travel before they were a safe distance from all
planetary bodies so there should be time to sleep. Diamond set
the computer to engage the drive automatically as soon as they
achieved minimum safe distance and went to select a cabin. By
the time she woke, they should be able to begin contacting their
old comrades and employees and friends, to let them know they
were still alive.

Tomorrow was going to be a long day.

When she woke, she sensed that the drive had activated in her
sleep. A quick glance through one of the glassteel windows confirmed her suspicion, as the familiar constellations of her favorite
system greeted her. She yawned and stretched, thankful that she
wouldn't have to spend an hour getting ready for the day. She no
longer had to ply on makeup to conceal the size of her eyes or
her *tress*. Out here, in her world, nobody would care that she was
an Emovete instead of a human. Well, part Emovete, but who was
counting? She certainly wasn't. Having larger than normal eyes
was more of a hindrance than a benefit, in her opinion, and having her *tress* visible all the time rather than only when she was
highly agitated could be even more of a liability. The only thing
she missed out on was the ability to see in the infrared spectrum,

present in her full-blooded brethren, but lacking in her for some reason.

Instead, she padded down the corridor to the bridge, where she found Knave, already waiting with his morning tea. A second cup, one she prayed was herbal, waited on her console.

His appearance had changed more drastically than hers had. He still had shaggy brown hair and deep brooding eyes, but the most revealing difference was in the quantity of eyes he now displayed. The exaggerated brow line, which had been necessary to camouflage the third eye in his forehead, was bare.

"So," she yawned again as she settled into her seat and inhaled the fruit-flavored steam wafting off her cup. "It looks like we've still got some work ahead of us."

He nodded his agreement, all three eyes focused on the screen in front of him. "Everything's been handed off."

"I figured as much." All of their assets, including their homes, ships, and wealth, even their command of the most effective troupe of pilferers, scam artists, and cat burglars known to the galaxy, had been distributed to their successors.

Their entire empire, one that they had painstakingly built from the ground up, was gone.

"If there's anything left in long-term storage," he said as her emotions began to falter, "We might still have something."

"Sure, but not much. If there is anything — and that's a big *if* — we might be able to start with a few credits, but not enough." Credits were the recognized intergalactic currency that most races did business in, so Knave and Diamond had used it as the standard for their own transactions and kept most of their funds in credit-based accounts.

"No," he agreed with her. "Not much at all. But it's a place to start."

She sighed and echoed his words, as close to an agreement as she could muster. *A place to start,* she thought to herself. *As if I haven't had to start over with nothing enough times already.*

She wondered how long it would take to regain the status that she had reached, and wondered if she had enough years left in her to claw back to the top, through ranks of people more skilled and more practiced than she was. Their time on Earth had definitely made a dent in their skill sets and although neither of them had said as much, they both knew that they would have to get back to their previous skill levels in a hurry if they wanted to stay competitive against everyone.

After all, she and Knave had trained most of them.

It had taken many years of trial and error, learning from more mistakes than either of them cared to admit, to rise from the lowest level of society to become a force to be reckoned with in the underground world they had chosen. Along the way, they had gathered similar like-minded people to join forces, all of them every bit as hungry for success as they themselves were. Slowly but with determination, Diamond and Knave had built an empire to be reckoned with. Twice as they grew, they had been forced to defend against someone who wanted to take the empire they were building by force, and twice they had rebuffed the attempt. Now, fighting for control a third time was almost inevitable.

Unless, of course, the worst had happened.

Although both of them were willing to discuss the possibility of having to retake control of the Deck, neither wanted to admit out loud that there was a good possibility that there would be no Deck left to take back. One small mistake could easily lead to the downfall of the entire organization, similarly to how the FBI had managed to track Knave and Diamond to one of their safehouses. Without their experience and their contacts to alert them to potential danger, those they had once led may have already been incarcerated as a reward for their efforts to continue the Deck's might.

"Are they still active?"

"Hard to tell," he answered without looking up from his screen. "Either they aren't doing much lately, or they have managed to keep everything really quiet and I'm not seeing any reports on them."

Silence from her former companions wasn't a good sign, as far as Diamond could tell. She mentally ran through the list of who was likely to take over the empire in their absence and while there were a handful of people who she believed could manage the Deck, they weren't likely to sustain against any attempts at coup. "What about our contacts? Anything left there?"

"Couple," he answered. "I can send out some feelers and see if we still have anyone friendly on the other side who's willing to work with us."

One of the biggest reasons for their success was the quantity of informants, cutting-edge goods sellers, and all-around bribe-takers they had developed throughout the years. Having the right person in the right place to ensure nobody was looking when they were going through an area, to inform them when something big was uncovered that could be profitable to the right people, or to let them know when the IG's forces were getting a little too close for comfort had been the most valuable assets in their arsenal. Without having those types of contacts, they would be going into most situations blindly, leaving them open to grievous mistakes.

"Let's just hope someone else isn't already paying them a whole lot more."

CALLING ALL CARDS

"So how do we want to play this?" Once again, Knave broke into her reverie, bringing her out of her thoughts and into reality. "We've got some options, so I think we need to decide what we want to do next."

Diamond knew that he was right. Their options may not have been good but at least they were present. "I think we need to start by finding out if we have anything left in long-term storage." It was as good of a place as any to start, no matter what they did from then on out. Whichever direction they went, they would need money and, just as importantly, they would need supplies.

"I'm already checking on it," he answered absently. "There's still a unit left on Majapa that looks like it hasn't been touched, but I'm not sure what is in it. Hopefully enough to get us started. Beyond that, I'm not sure yet." He looked at her askance. "What about the Deck? Do we want to try getting back in touch with them?"

She snarled in frustration. "What do you think I've been trying to do?" she demanded. "I've called every face card we had in the Deck but none of them are still active." Because of their particular names and that their troupe had been called the Deck, Diamond and Knave had developed a system of ranking their members based on a standard deck of playing cards from one of the worlds they had visited during their youth, an idea that had initially started as a joke but had grown in popularity among their friends and associates quickly so they had continued the practice. Within the hierarchy she had designed, face cards were assigned to the officers, and these were the most likely people to have taken control once she and Knave were no longer available to lead. "None of their numbers are still active."

It had tickled her plenty when she discovered that playing cards had existed on the planet they had just vacated and she had amassed a collection of them during their exile, for no better reason than because they reminded her of home and she wanted them. Most of her collection had been left behind but a few of her favorites were packed in with the rest of her belongings.

In the early days of the Deck, some had questioned why Knave was ranked so much lower than the Queen of Diamonds when they were obviously equals within the organization, but his answer had always been that he preferred that card over any others he could be assigned. Besides, he liked to keep the appearance that Diamond was solely in charge. Also unbeknownst to most members of the Deck and their associates, they weren't truly partners in the sense of both having equal responsibility over their empire. From the beginning, the Deck had been Diamond's dream and Knave simply felt it was his duty to ensure her success. Diamond was the queen of her empire, both by card designation and by role within the organization. Nobody was higher ranked than she.

"What about the rest of the suits?" he asked, clearly surprised by her news. There should have been some face cards left, even if some of them had retired. To be able to reach *none* of them was unusual indeed. "Have you tried them?"

Below the face cards, the foot soldiers of the operation were ranked on a number system following the standard playing card format from two to ten, where ten was the highest rank a member of the Deck could reach before becoming a face card. Before they had been stranded on Earth, there had been well over a hundred numbered cards in their organization. Now, she was beginning to wonder if there was a single one left.

"Working on it." Her voice was filled with exasperation as she answered. "But there's only so many contacts I can remember off the top of my head. The ones I called the most often were the ones I started with."

"Don't yell at me," he answered defensively, his hands in the air, palm-out in the universal gesture of surrender. "I wasn't criticizing."

"I know." She looked from the communication monitor before her over to where he sat at a similar bank of controls. She sighed and lowered her voice to a more reasonable volume. "I know. But this worries me."

Between the pair of them, they managed to come up with a scant handful of lower-ranked cards that she could try to contact. Again, she was met with the same "out of service" message she had received previously but, when there were only two numbers left on the list, she finally found an active number.

"Who is this?" demanded the voice on the other end of the line. "This is for secure communications only."

"Is this the Four of Hearts?" Diamond asked, unfazed by the woman's hostile greeting.

"You tell me," the voice retorted. "Is that who you're trying to call?" The voice was slightly nasal, as though the speaker suffered from allergies or had a head cold.

"Excellent," Diamond said. "You are just the person I wanted to talk to."

"Look," the Four of Hearts interrupted her. "If you're trying to sell something, you've called the wrong department. Other than that, you need to get off my comm."

Diamond sighed. She hadn't known this card personally, so she wasn't sure how temperamental the woman had been twelve years previously, but the conversation was swiftly getting nowhere. "This is the Queen of Diamonds," she snapped, her voice full of authority. "Any communication from me is automatically considered priority."

There was silence on the other end of the line, followed by a peal of laughter. "Seriously," she said between heaving breaths, "Whoever this is, you'd better not let the Aces know you're spreading rumors like that." Her voice sobered. "Besides, it isn't funny. The Queen of Diamonds is dead. This is not a good idea for a practical joke."

"I assure you," Diamond responded, her voice as calm as she could maintain it, "I'm not dead and this is no joke."

It took almost twenty minutes for her to convince the Four that she was indeed who she claimed to be. Four's responses slowly shifted from disbelief to amazement to excitement. "Does this mean you plan to take control of the Deck again?" she asked, hope ringing in her voice.

"That's what we're trying to determine," Diamond answered her. "We need to figure out who is in charge now, because the people we left in control seem to be out of contact."

Her statement and its implied question were met with a lengthy silence on the other end of the comm. "They're gone," Four answered at long last. "They're all gone."

"Gone?" the news stunned Diamond and even Knave, who had been listening in on the conversation, seemed surprised. "What do you mean gone?" She hoped that the woman meant retired, but the tone of her voice said volumes otherwise. "Where are they?"

"There... there was a coup," Four explained with a hesitant voice. "Shortly after you were declared dead, there was a coup in the ranks. One of the captains – I think he was a Nine or a Ten – made a play for control."

Diamond hissed between her teeth, wondering when a Nine could be considered a captain and curious as to who this mystery person had been. She would soon find out; members who had achieved the rank of Nine had made names for themselves and she would be able to recognize the person once she identified who he was. "What happened next?"

"He declared himself the King of Clubs. He brought in mercenaries," Four explained, "and assassins. They took over everything."

"And what happened to my commanders?" Diamond asked, her voice far gentler than the expression on her face and in her body posturing would otherwise indicate. Of all the outcomes that could have happened after her and Knave's exile, that was about the worst she had imagined. She wasn't surprised, however, as many similar organizations to hers had operated with mercenaries for one reason or another. Now she just needed to know how deep this change went.

"We didn't have a choice." Four was openly sobbing. "The only options we had were to obey the new order or be killed, too."

"So, they didn't retire." It wasn't so much a question as a statement of the obvious.

"No," Four confirmed. "There's no retirement anymore. The only way to get out of the Deck is dead."

"Was there no resistance?" Knave spoke up for the first time since their identities had been established. "Those cards were too well trained to have given in without a fight."

"Yeah, there was resistance, but it didn't last for very long. Everyone who went against the new leadership were declared traitors and they all started to disappear. Now, he doesn't even try to hide the fact that he uses Aces as his own private hit squad.

"They do what they're told, and they can't be bribed; I know plenty of cards who tried."

Four continued to answer Diamond and Knave's questions as well as she was able. At only the rank of a four, there wasn't a lot of information the woman had that was of much help about the inner workings of the Deck, but the information she did have was devastating. Even in Diamond's worst fears, she had never imagined anything this catastrophic.

The thing that Diamond abhorred even more than drugs was violence. She had seen far too much of it in her lifetime, so the first thing that she and Knave had agreed upon was that there would be no violence within the Deck. There were some overly aggressive people who got out of line every now and again and Diamond was certain that there were some small in-person fights every so often, but as a whole the Deck was a peaceful organization. Anyone who became too problematic was deemed a risk to the entire organization and was either retired or turned over to the authorities to handle.

Over the years, many people had suggested to them that they should employ some mercenaries as a defensive force only, but Diamond had stood firm. That was one of the main reasons why, despite the amount of larceny they partook in, nobody was particularly anxious to attack and dismantle them. There were far bigger groups with many more members out in the galaxy for them to spend their efforts on, groups that posed a very real and substantial threat to the population. By remaining peaceful, the Deck had remained under the radar, at least as far as threats to their safety was concerned.

Cardiss, the system that she and Knave had called home for most of their adult lives, had been perfect for their endeavors. Diamond even thought that it was remarkable that the system's name was similar to her own organization, and she loved the auditory pun involved in basing their operation in Cardiss. In return, the planets of the Cardiss system had welcomed them and allowed their group to prosper, understanding that their activities brought much to the local economy and that the planets within the system as a whole were not under threat. Out of respect to their neighbors, the Deck performed no thefts or other similar activities in their system.

Now, Cardiss and many of the surrounding systems now lived in a state of constant fear of the Deck and in particular terror of the newly-murderous Aces.

The Nine of Clubs, who had now declared himself to be the King of Clubs, had usurped command in their absence and turned their peaceful, if larcenous, acquisitions organization into an instrument of terror.

THE DESPAIR OF FUTILITY

Knave and Diamond sat back at the news, appalled at what they had just heard. There was no point in asking any further questions about what had been done to their people and with their empire in their absence; they had already learned far more than they needed to. They looked at each other in shock.

Something had to be done.

"Is there anyone loyal left?" Diamond asked after a lengthy silence. Her voice echoed the doubts that Knave was feeling as well. Under violence such as what their people had already been through, residual loyalty wasn't likely to be in high supply.

"There are some," the Four of Hearts reassured them after an equally lengthy pause. "I'm not sure how many, though."

The news, bad as it sounded, was better than they could have hoped for. No matter what the odds, some was always better than none. "Loyal?" Knave asked, "or just unhappy?"

"It doesn't matter," Diamond spoke up before Four could answer. Regardless of whether there were people who were loyal to Diamond and Knave and all they had believed in or whether they were simply unhappy with the new regime, she understood that assets were assets. "How many of them can you get in contact with?"

"I'm not sure," Four answered with hesitation in her voice. "I would have to do some searching to see how many there are first."

"Good enough." Diamond picked up her almost-forgotten cup of herbal tea and took a sip as she thought. Even though it was no longer hot, it was better than nothing. "Contact as many as you can," she finally said as she put the cup back down. "We'll let you know further in a few days." Without waiting for a response, she pressed the button to end the call.

"We need to figure out a meeting place," Knave said as Diamond broke the connection.

"I know," she responded absently, picking up her cup and taking another drink of her cooled tea. "Maybe on one of the space stations. There's usually plenty of room for private conversations there."

"True," he looked at her, his brows lowered in concern. He didn't have to ask how she was feeling after the call. Jagged lines had begun creeping down her arms and up her neck, beginning as pale brown stripes but darkening to dull red, as though lightning had broken out within her body and was reaching for escape.

This *tress*, even more than the size of her eyes, showed the quantity of Emovete blood running through Diamond's veins. She was not completely of the Emovete line, otherwise the markings would always be visible. She was half at best, and a quarter at the least.

The *tress* themselves weren't uncomfortable for Diamond, as Knave well knew. Instead, they served as a warning to those around her. As with all other Emovetes, the lines represented strong emotions, a physical depiction of something most people kept hidden deep inside. On Earth, she had kept the traces of her heritage concealed beneath extensive training in self-calming techniques and layers of makeup. On the few rare occasions where the lines had become visible through even the thick concealer she wore, she had laughed it off as an old tattoo that she regretted. Because tattoos, regrettable tattoos in particular, were so common among the Earthlings, her explanation had always been accepted without a second thought.

Now, her markings were blazing a deep, furious red. She hadn't bothered with makeup that morning and no amount of deep breathing could quell her fury. For as calm as she had kept her voice during the conversation with Four, and as much as she held her poise, there was no denying that she was raging inside.

"A station rendezvous isn't a very good idea," Knave said. "If these people are as prone to violence as Four said they were – and we have no reason to doubt what she said – they won't hesitate to blow up a station if they suspect what we're up to." He had long had a penchant for moving towards the worst-case scenarios in any given situation, a mindset that had kept both of them alive far more often than either of them wanted to consider. Normally this mentality was a point of contention between them, but in this case, it seemed entirely warranted and not in the slightest way unreasonable.

Diamond forced herself to calm, to think rationally. Knave's words rang true, and she recognized the fallacy in her logic immediately: Just because *she* would never order the destruction of a space station, that didn't mean that others would hold the same regard for intelligent life. She had seen enough even in her brief lifetime to know that much was true. There were an amazing number of people who had no problem throwing away sentient lives for the smallest of reasons... as long as those lives weren't their own. From what they had just discovered, it seemed like the people now in control of the Deck were every bit as callous and inhumane as those she had known long ago, possibly even worse.

"So where do you recommend?" She asked as she took another drink of the tea, thankful for yet another reason that it was an herbal blend rather than one of his blacks. The last thing she needed was caffeine at that particular moment.

"A lunar base would be better."

She looked over at him in surprise. Knave had never been fond of lunar bases, and after their entrapment on Earth, she had expected him to be unwilling, at the least, to set foot on another planetary surface for quite some time yet. While a moon didn't qualify as a planet, per se, it was close enough. "Why?"

"Harder to destroy," he shrugged one shoulder noncommittally. "It's easy to wipe out a solitary station, floating out in its orbit. Anything attached to a planet, or even a planetoid like a moon, is going to be a lot harder to take out completely.

"Besides," he grimaced as he stretched his back into an awkward, uncomfortable angle, "Supplies are easier to get on lunar bases than anywhere else."

"But space stations have defenses that lunar bases don't." Her argument was weak, and she knew it.

"Maybe against attack from outside," he admitted, "but stations are usually a lot more focused on defending against meteorites and small objects like that; most of them don't have much by way of defense against deliberate attacks. Unless, of course, you were thinking of going to a military station." He raised his brows at her questioningly, although both of them knew that idea was out of the question. "Neither of them has anything to prevent an attack within. And lunar bases have a surface beneath them that they're anchored to, so having one suddenly floating off, powerless, through space is much less likely."

Diamond looked down at her tea and swirled the miniscule amount of liquid that remained at the bottom of the cup listlessly. Her anger had faded almost as swiftly as it had risen so all that was left was a deep, aching sense of despair. "It's all over, isn't it?" she muttered as she watched the peach-colored whirlpool.

"Why do you say that?"

"We can't take over our old headquarters," she said without meeting any of his eyes. The entire time they had been trapped on Earth, her constant hope was to someday return to their old lives in one shape or another. They had both realized there would be a time of transition when they returned, but neither had really considered the possibility of not having anything at all to return to.

Well, she considered, *maybe Knave had.* He tended to think about things like that far more often than she did, and probably a lot more often than he told her about.

"Why not?" She could feel his gaze on her, even without looking up. "We built that place from the ground up. Who knows it better than we do?"

"He has assassins," she sighed in exasperation. "By now, they'll have explored the entire compound. We can't rely on any of our passages still being undiscovered." She finally looked up to meet his stare with only the slightest hint of tears shining in her eyes. "Found, at best. Trapped is far more likely."

He breathed between his teeth, a low whistling sound. "Well then, if we can't go back, what do you think we should do?" Seeing her upset was always a motivation for him to find a way to make things better. He had been like that since the day they met. He would do just about anything to take the weight of sadness and despair from her shoulders, just as he had done from the moment they had met. Many times over the intervening years, he had seen her in low spirits but never like this. Today, she appeared to have simply accepted that she had lost everything for good. He needed to shift her vision from the bleak outlook she currently saw to a plan, a way of moving back towards the life she knew, the life she deserved. She needed motivation, and he could help with that.

"We need a new base."

"That's a reasonable place to start." He lifted her cup out of her hand and walked across the small room to refill it. "Then what?"

"People," Diamond answered. "No operation can run without people, and there are only two of us."

"What about Four?" He inquired as he set the steaming cup in front of her. "She makes three, and that's not even counting anyone else she brings with her."

"Three isn't much better than two," she countered. "But that's a good point." She picked up the drink and blew gently at the steam. "Maybe there's more than just a couple of our old crew that we can wrench away from the King of Clubs and his assassins."

He nodded encouragingly. "If we can get enough of them onto our side, it will disrupt the balance. The staff at the lowest levels is the base. Without them, the hierarchy can become unstable.

"But there's a bigger problem."

His last comment drew her attention away from her tea. "How can there possibly be a bigger problem?" She swung her hands wide, almost sloshing her tea in the process. "Isn't all of this bad enough?"

He clicked on a control panel, causing one of the monitors to light up before her. Frustrated, she set the cup down and read the text as it appeared. As she read, her eyebrows raised higher and higher, until they looked like they would crawl off her face completely. By the time she reached the end of the message, her hands were visibly shaking.

Due to the increasingly violent activity in and around the Cardiss system, she read, *requests have been sent to the Interplanetary Government for assistance.* "Have they sent out Triad yet?" she whispered in horror.

"It doesn't look like it," Knave reassured her. "But it's bound to happen soon." He paused for a moment before adding, "Unless they already have, and we just don't know it yet."

She had reason to fear. Triad, the military arm of the Interplanetary Government, was known for being swift, dangerous, uncompromising, and unstoppable. In fact, chances were high that Triad had already been called to action over the Deck's movements.

They were just good enough to keep anyone from noticing it.

If the forces of Triad had been called to arms in the past, there had been a chance, however slight, that the Deck was capable of withstanding their troops, if only for a little while. Even now, where the Deck had teams of mercenaries, they might be able to hold out against the initial assault. With their current resources, however, Diamond held no illusions on her chances with Triad without the safety of the Deck; she knew that she and Knave held no such chance. Triad had thousands upon thousands of troops, including full teams of highly trained soldiers who specialized in routing groups just like the Deck. In fact, Triad's special forces teams had already been credited with taking out three of Diamond's most violent offenders, which had served as both a relief and a warning.

Knave had been right. This was indeed a bigger problem. Apparently just dealing with the King of Clubs and his force of assassins and mercenaries wasn't enough of a challenge. They also needed to find a way to keep Triad at bay.

Once again, Diamond sunk her head into the fold of her arms in despair. This time, she didn't bother trying to keep the tears of frustration from overflowing. The best scenario she could see, at least for the moment, was for Triad to eliminate the entire Deck. That would leave absolutely nothing to stand in Diamond's way, but it also eliminated any potential allies she may have developed within the King of Clubs's organization as well. Additionally, if and when she rebuilt her own empire, she would have to completely change everything about it. Once Triad got a group in their sights, they monitored to ensure that no trace of them ever resurfaced.

With this latest development, there was simply no way to win. Even if she did manage to overthrow the new leader of the Deck, she would be left defenseless against the military.

"I have a suggestion." Knave's voice was calming, soothing even, "but you're not going to like it." Diamond mumbled something incomprehensible without looking up. He continued as though he understood what she had said. "How likely do you think it is that the King continued sending baskets?"

She lifted her head barely enough to peer at him over her arms, barely holding in a snicker of derision. "There's no way. Nobody else knew what those were for."

"Exactly." His grin widened. "And if he didn't know, he wouldn't have kept them up."

"Or if he had," She continued his train of thought, "they would have changed." She took a deep, calming breath and worked on settling her emotions. There was hope in the idea. A delivery to the leader of Triad, Commander Ryan Moore, would catch their attention and alert them that something had changed. If they could find the right kind of items to include with the basket, it might even give them enough leeway to start their overhaul of the Deck. It just might give them the breathing space she needed.

"There's a problem with that, though."

"Oh?" Knave raised his central eyebrow in curiosity.

"We've never sent a basket to Commander Moore," she reminded him. "Ever. They probably wouldn't know what to make of it either." *Even worse*, she thought without putting voice to the idea, *they might take it as a declaration of intent.*

Knave didn't seem as bothered by the idea as she was. "Triad's probably the most successful group out there, right?" When she agreed, he continued. "And we both know that for a force to be both that large and that successful there has to be a ton of information flooding through it, at all levels. They'd have to have information-gathering units everywhere, collecting every bit of data they can find on everything they possibly can.

"With the increase of hostilities over the last dozen or so years, I'd lay pretty good odds that Triad's been doing as much research as they can on the Deck and what they've been known to do, both historically and more recently.

"They probably already recognize that something happened, something big, which changed what the Deck did when the King of Clubs took control. Better, their research would have shown them that we used to give the baskets, and then stopped."

"Do you really think that, by us sending them one now, they'll recognize what it means?"

He nodded. "I wouldn't be at all surprised if they have examples of baskets we'd sent out years ago. Not the baskets themselves, of course, but details on what the baskets contained. Probably even holo files of the originals."

Diamond nodded as well, considering the possibilities. If they were wrong and sent a basket anyway, it could prove disastrous. On the other hand, however, if Knave was right, it could open a dialogue of a sort and let Triad know that they were back to clean up the mess that had been made in their absence.

As if there had been any real question about it. Both her and Knave's existences were based on the toss of the dice.

A ROCK, A HARD PLACE, AND
A PSIONIST

The Four of Hearts agreed to the meeting. Well before the arranged time, the Queen of Diamonds and Knave of Spades were in place on the moon base.

As far as lunar bases went, at least in Diamond's opinion, this one wasn't too bad. She had seen some truly squalid bases during her travels and had often wondered how people could stand to live in such circumstances. When Knave had first recommended setting up the meeting on a lunar base, Diamond's mind had immediately been filled with visions of a hostile and cold environment, where everything was stark and unwelcoming.

The one that Knave selected for their meeting, in comparison to Diamond's fertile imagination, was fantastic. It was a bit sparse, which was no big surprise considering that its main purpose was to act as a transport hub for the salt mines on the moon's surface. Most of the people that frequented the base, therefore, were either miners or cargo haulers, neither of which had much use for formalities.

There was, to Diamond's relief, a passable restaurant with a decent bar. The restaurant was as unpretentious as the rest of the base, and rather than the exotic fare that some of the other bases advertised, it served only hearty, filling meals.

That was fine with Diamond, as the only foods she had eaten for over a decade were Earth-based meals and it had been far too long since she had eaten even the simplest of native foods. Although there were food supplies on the ship they had stolen, they were all designed for long distance travel and required rehydration, nowhere near as appetizing as fresh food. Here, finally, she could enjoy a proper meal.

They waited at the bar for their guests. The bar carried a brew that was similar to the thick, heady beers that Knave had developed a taste for on Earth and he drained his third glass before anyone arrived. They didn't have any of the herbal teas that Diamond had grown accustomed to, but they had one of her old favorite flavors of wine, which she was more than pleased about.

Just before the appointed time, a young-looking Emovete walked cautiously into the bar. Unlike Diamond, who was the product of multiple races, the newcomer had deep brown eyes that were easily twice the size of Diamond's own oversized orbs. Dark brown streaks covered most of her visible skin; her arms, neck, and even parts of her face were streaked with the telltale markings. Where Diamond's *tress* became pale enough to match her skin tone when her emotions were calm, full-blooded Emovetes always had visible markings.

As her eyes fell on Diamond and Knave, a flicker of color ran through her *tress,* echoing the fear and relief that played across her face.

She was followed into the dimly-lit pub by six others. Four of her companions were humanoid, but it was impossible to tell to which particular race they belonged. Many of the inhabited planets that were known throughout the universe had human and human-looking populations and many of the races were virtually indistinguishable from one another.

The fifth person to enter the bar was a Tet, the same race as Knave. He was taller than the Knave of Spades, and more heavily muscled, but all three of his eyes looked warily at Knave as he strode across the room.

Diamond was surprised to see him but she fought to keep the surprise from showing. Tets were, for the most part, vicious and battle-thirsty. Outcasts such as Knave were few and far between, as not many who turned against the principles of their dominant brethren survived to walk away. Either this Tet was much better at guarding himself from the violence that famed his people or he was a mercenary and personified the violence that Diamond wanted to avoid.

The last to follow Four into the room was even less human-looking than any of the others. They were short, less than a unit tall at the tips of their tall, pointed ears, but squat. Wrinkles of grey flesh poured down their body like wax from a melting candle, puddling into a mass that almost rubbed against the floor as they waddled on three feet that were barely visible beneath the rest of their body. This was a Dolrathi, a race known for the vast amounts of intelligence that each of them held in their small, unimpressive-looking bodies.

Their eyes were solid black and seemed to absorb whatever light struck them. Rumors about the Dolrathi's ability to simply *look* at something and immediately know all about it had never been denied, and seeing how this particular Dolrathi seemed to absorb everything within eyesight led Diamond to wonder if the rumors might be true after all.

At the very least, she reasoned to herself, she understood from where the rumors had originated.

Whatever else the Dolrathi may be, they were creepy.

"Come, friends," Knave said as soon as the group was close enough that he wouldn't have to shout. "Join us for a meal."

Relief washed over the humans' faces, but the Dolrathi and Tet remained unreadable. All of them accepted a chair and, at Knave's insistence, ordered lunch.

"So," Diamond spoke up once everyone had a chance to order and calm down for a moment, "I would like to know more about what's been happening in my absence."

Four sent her a weak smile and bowed her head slightly. "Other than what we discussed earlier," she said hesitantly, "what do you want to know?"

"I want to know more about how things are being run." She met each of their eyes squarely. "I understand that a card calling himself the King of Clubs is behind all of it."

"Yes, that's true."

"Do you know what rank he held before he promoted himself?"

The group looked around the table at each other, as though trying to decide who would speak up. Finally, it was the Dolrathi who answered. "He was a Club." Their voice was calm and clear. "I was not aware of him before he became King but I believe he was a Nine."

Diamond nodded slowly. All of her cards, members of the Deck, had been ranked first by suit and then by number. The lower the number was, the less power and responsibility that person held. Conversely, for a card to attain the levels of ten or above, he or she must have done something to prove either their loyalty or their prowess – usually both.

When she asked for a description of the man, each of the visitors looked at each other blankly. "We've never seen him," the Dolrathi answered finally. "He sends out his Aces when he needs something or to issue orders. He doesn't deal with any of us directly."

Diamond had known all of her face cards by sight but that didn't help her now. If he had only been a nine, it was unlikely that he had drawn her attention. She had no photographs or other images of any of her former associates, let alone the man now calling himself King, but she ran through a mental tally of every Club she could remember. If he had been a ten when she had left, there were about fifty different people he could have been. Nines, on the other hand, were far more plentiful.

Plus, she realized the possibility that he had been even lower ranked when she and Knave had landed on Earth; he may have been promoted in her absence, in which case none of the fifty she had come up with would be he.

"Tell me about his assassins."

"Well," Four cleared her throat. "All of them are Aces, at least all of them that I've heard of. They're scattered through all of the suits and nobody says anything against them."

"Of course." Aces, it would seem, had changed in their absence as well. Once upon a time, the Aces had been spies, specifically tasked with getting information and finding weaknesses where there were believed to be none. From a twisted mindset such as the one possessed by the person calling himself the King of Clubs, it could be rationalized that moving from spies to assassins was the natural progression.

"What about us?" Diamond asked. "Who are the standing Queen of Diamonds and Knave of Spades?" The question was irrelevant, strategically. Because there were only a set number of suit and rank positions within the Deck, and because there were more members of the Deck than individual identities to give them, there would always be multiple people in each rank. Her question stemmed from nothing more than curiosity and a small amount of vanity.

"Nobody." The Tet's deep, basso voice was the first to respond. "He tried, once," he explained as both Diamond and Knave raised eyebrows in curiosity, "but there was too much of an outcry over it. Your ranks have been retired."

Slowly, the others began to join in the conversation as Diamond and Knave peppered them with questions. Even the obviously hesitant humans added their ideas and thoughts into the matter.

The Deck, they discovered, hadn't been satisfied with taking complete control of Cardiss. They had expanded to the next two systems in one direction, maintaining almost complete control of Xerxes and still fighting for control in Yareth. In the other direction, Zedoin had fallen quickly under their assault, no big surprise. Zedoin had always been a peaceful system of planets and Diamond's blood boiled at the thought of the passive, complacent Zedoese falling prey to the predatory Deck.

Because of this expansion, the Deck had increased its numbers to a point unimaginable by previous standards. Where Diamond had maintained a standing crew of hundreds, the King of Clubs now ruled over thousands.

No, she corrected herself, it was more than that.

Hundreds of thousands.

Perhaps they could withstand Triad after all, suggested the nagging voice in the back of her mind.

"The Clubs scare and intimidate everyone," one of the obviously frightened humans explained. "After we take over a planet, they gather up everyone who looks like they can fight. They force everyone to join the Deck, whether they want to or not, and then they use them as cannon fodder wherever there's fighting to be done."

"The face cards still lead everything," another human added, "but they're pretty much all loyal to the King." When Knave inquired as to whether they were loyal due to fear or other means, he explained. "It's a little bit of both, I think. All of the face cards had been given much larger holdings than you guys allotted for them. So long as they do what they're told, they get to keep everything and stay in power. Those who don't... well, they get demoted and become just more cannon fodder."

The news kept getting worse. Diamond had expected that the cards would continue their acquisition and sales activities as normal, just more aggressively than had been done while she had still been in charge. What she was quite displeased to discover that they had moved part of their operation into a previously prohibited area: the manufacture and distribution of Roxxy.

Roxxy was one of the most potent and addictive substances available on the black market. While it fetched a handsome price, Diamond had always refused to enter into business with any organization or individual that made, used, or sold it. Now, her team was the leading source of the horrid drug. She couldn't help but look back at all of the efforts she had made to rid Earth of its drugs, only to discover that her own people were now even worse. Unfortunately, none of those who had come to their meeting knew where the drug was being manufactured.

Knave and Diamond sent them back to their posts once the discussion ended, asking them to spread the word among those who were still loyal to them about their return. "This will end," she promised them. "I will make sure of it."

"Check your tracking beacons," Knave said as all of them stood to leave, "and have the others do so as well. When we give you the call, the beacons on your ships will need to be removed as soon as possible.

"When we call, we'll tell you where to meet. Dismantle your trackers and move as quickly as you can." He blinked slowly and looked at their small gathering of followers.

"We will provide the distraction."

Once their erstwhile followers left, Diamond let the brave face dissolve. "This is awful," she moaned as Knave slid another drink in front of her. "How much worse is it going to get?"

"Just stay calm," he reassured her as he took a drink of his own ale. "You can't hold yourself responsible for everything that happened in the Deck while you were gone."

"I know that," she sniffed as she took a sip, relieved that it wasn't the yeasty-flavored beer that he was drinking. "I told them I could fix it." She looked up to meet his eyes. "But I'm just not sure I can this time."

"Sure, you can," he reassured her. "You have done more things that nobody else would've thought possible than anyone I've ever met; this is nowhere near as challenging as some of the stuff you've already done."

She could tell that he was worried as well, although he was fighting to keep her from knowing it. When she called him on it, he didn't try to deny it.

"Of course, I'm worried," he chuckled. "But not about the same things you are." She arched an eyebrow at him, so he explained, his voice much calmer and more serious than usual.

"I'm worried about the promise I made to you. Right now, I can't deny that we're at war – or at least, soon to be – and I promised that you'd never have to fight for your survival again."

He took a long pull from his beer before continuing. "I plan to keep that promise for as long as I'm alive, but I'm worried about what might happen to you once I'm gone."

Diamond shook her head fiercely while he was still talking, not even wanting to entertain the idea of having to continue without him, her best friend, the closest thing she had ever had to an older brother. For that matter, he was the closest thing she had ever had to a family at all.

"We'll need to find a good place for our base of operations," she said, and he accepted the change in subject without argument.

"What about moles?" he asked. "You know as well as I do that as soon as someone finds out we're setting up a resistance, they're going to send in spies of their own."

"I know," she admitted, "but I'm not sure how to find them right now."

"Can I make a suggestion?"

"Of course." She looked up at him in surprise. Knave knew that his suggestions and recommendations were always welcome, so asking for permission was out of the ordinary. This could only mean that he had something unusual up his sleeve. Her eyes narrowed in suspicion.

"We need a psionist."

Psionists were people with the ability to see into the mind of another, with or without their consent. Diamond had maintained a large network of them while she had been in charge of the Deck but that had been long ago. "We don't have any, remember?" she responded. "At least not ones we know we can trust."

"What if we look outside the Deck for one?"

Diamond's heart sank as she realized where he was going. She had never liked working with Protus, but she couldn't deny that the man was good. He had at one time been offered a position within the Deck, a position he had refused in order to remain completely freelance. While he was willing to accept contract work on occasion, he much preferred to make his own rules and live by his own schedule, a mindset which Diamond could respect.

If only he didn't get on her nerves so much.

"And, just to be sure," knowing what her objections would be, Knave continued, "We can have him check out the ones that we just met with to be sure that they are all trustworthy, too."

"Are you sure we can trust him, though?" She sighed, knowing the answer even before she asked it. Obnoxious as he may be, the one thing Protus could be relied on was honesty. Brutal, knife-edged honesty, that was certain, but honesty nevertheless. "Fine. Call him."

"We'll need a secondary base," she said, almost as an after-thought. "Somewhere to put the moles."

The Knave of Spades looked up at her with interest. "What are you planning?"

"I'm thinking that spies only work if they have information to pass. We tell them that the base we're sending them to will be the primary information hub, so they think they've got the inside track. Everyone else can go to the other base, which is where the actual activities and decisions will be made."

"I see," his eyes widened in surprise at the simple logic of it all. "We send misleading information to the moles, so we know what the Deck knows."

"Exactly." She smiled a feral grin at him. "Misinformation; smoke and mirrors. As long as they get enough valid information, they won't suspect that we already know what they're up to."

"Valid information?"

She nodded. "Technically, it's still valid even if it is a little late."

VERY SPECIAL DELIVERY

"Here are your reports," Brian Coffee smiled as he set a stack of papers on the edge of Commander Moore's desk. He placed a mug of coffee next to the stack, knowing which of his two deliveries held the highest priority in his boss's eyes.

Ryan Moore, commander of Triad, smiled gratefully up at his assistant, looking even more tired than he had the morning previously. Faint lines had begun to appear on his normally smooth face, a sure sign of the stress he had been under lately. He stood in front of a wall of windows, looking out into the misty morning.

Beyond the windows, the city of Midway woke as well, far below the soaring height of the Triad Towers, a trio of buildings which each stood over a hundred stories tall. The towers were in the center of the city, which in turn filled the massive island upon which it had been built and after which it had been named. Members of Triad had been the first intelligent life on the planet and had developed the first civilization there. Every morning, Ryan stood at the windows of his office, far above street level and almost even with the clouds, to remind himself of exactly how far his people had come since their inception, and how much everyone still depended on him. Seventy percent of the planet's inhabitants were either a member themselves or were related to a member of Triad, and the weight of those millions of people was a constant pressure on his wide shoulders.

As usual, Commander Moore was dressed in clothing that was formal enough to wear to a business meeting but casual enough to be comfortable in. Soft, comfortable trousers and a well-loved blue button down with the collar unbuttoned and sleeves rolled up to the elbow were his preferred uniform for days at the office, with laced running shoes instead of formal shoes. As with most of the ranking officers of Triad, "desk-pushers," as some of the lower-ranked men liked to refer to them, Ryan was no longer required to wear his uniform every day. The only time he pulled it out of his closet was when he had to go out on personal inspections of the troops, and that was more because the troops demanded it than personal choice.

His sand-colored hair, which was not quite dark enough to be brown but not light enough to be blond, was short and trim; a style that suited his lean muscle and square jaw. The barest hint of a curl showed in the slightly longer hair on top of his head, indicating he was in need of a trip to the barber again.

"Any news from Cardiss?" he asked as soon as he downed half of the cup.

"Right here on top, sir." Coffee laid a hand on the top file, which was marked with a red priority tag. He waited for Ryan to finish the cup before adding, "And there's something else you need to see." Unlike Ryan's casual attire, Coffee preferred to wear suits, even though he had been informed multiple times that it wasn't necessary. Today's selection was a charcoal grey affair with a modest burgundy tie and matching pocket handkerchief. It was one of his favorites, custom-tailored as were most of his clothes.

Ryan raised an eyebrow, not so much in surprise as in curiosity. Coffee had been his aide, his personal assistant, and most importantly one of his closest friends for the better part of thirty years, so Ryan understood from his tone more than his words that, whatever he was talking about, it would be interesting. He set the empty cup down on the desk.

"What's that?"

Without answering, Coffee turned and left the room. He walked back in a moment later, carrying a large box. "It's already passed through all of the safety protocols," he reassured Ryan as he opened the top of the box to reveal its contents. "Everyone assures me that it's safe."

"Hmm." Ryan evaluated the box thoughtfully without peering inside. "I didn't know I was expecting any packages today." There was no information on the box to indicate from where it was sent, which aroused no small amount of suspicion. Although Coffee had reassured him that it had been thoroughly inspected, he couldn't help but be skeptical.

"You weren't," Coffee reassured him. "This is, I believe, a gift."

Ryan was naturally suspicious of gifts, especially impersonally-given ones. There had been far too many times where death had come calling packaged in friendly overtures for him to feel anything but unease at the box before him.

However, it wouldn't do for his men to see him hesitant, even if it was just Coffee and even if it was with good cause. If Coffee said the package was safe, there was no doubting it. Had there been anything even remotely threatening inside, the box would have been detonated without ever reaching the top floor of the Triad Towers.

Sensing his Commander's hesitation, Coffee reached into the box and extracted the contents. A wide, shallow basket formed of bright red, yellow, and blue woven wicker strips had once been wrapped in opaque yellow cellophane. The cellophane had been removed at some point during the package's inspection, and a large green satin bow with a good dozen loops in it was placed onto the desk next to the basket.

The basket contained more than just plastic and ribbon, Ryan discovered as curiosity overrode apprehension and he leaned forward to look at it more closely. There were fruits inside, some of which he recognized but many that he did not. What really got his attention, however, was the signature card.

Rather than the standard cards that usually arrived with such gifts, this one had a pair of cards. Playing cards, to be precise: the queen of diamonds and the knave of spades.

Ryan pulled the pair of playing cards out of the basket to examine them further, looking over at Coffee in surprise. "I thought they stopped this practice a long time ago." There were other items included in the basket as well: a news clipping about the request for Triad assistance in the Cardiss system and a glittering, rainbow-colored sticker in the shape of the universally-accepted peace symbol.

"They had," Coffee confirmed as he refilled Ryan's empty coffee cup from a freshly brewed carafe that lived on a table just inside his office door. "There hasn't been a single reported delivery such as this in over ten years."

"Ten years, hmm?" Commander Moore mused as he looked more thoughtfully at the basket and its contents. Suddenly, he lifted up the playing cards again and his eyes widened in surprise. "I need the original files," he snapped. "Now. Everything we've got on them, I want it in front of me."

As Coffee saluted and left, Ryan turned his attention to the files that had already been brought in that morning. As he read through them, his eyes and his mind continued to wander back to the basket, which was now sitting on the far edge of his desk, leaving him enough room to work. Much as he wanted to focus his attention on the mysterious gift, there was official business to attend to first.

It didn't take long for Coffee to return, this time bearing a handful of old, dusty files. Commander Moore picked up the stack of files that he had only just finished with and offered them to his assistant in return for the new stack.

"Sir?" Coffee stopped, his hand on the doorknob. "Should I leave word that you are not to be disturbed?"

"No," Ryan answered absently, already opening the first of the files. "If something important comes up, let me know." He barely noticed as the door swung shut on well-oiled hinges, leaving him to peruse the files in privacy.

As he read, he discovered how much had changed in the organization known as the Deck. The previous leaders, a pair of people known only as the Queen of Diamonds and the Knave of Spades, had for some unfathomable reason seen the need to name all of their agents after playing cards, themselves included.

The group had long been known for their policy of non-violence, a policy that had been completely disregarded a dozen or so years ago. As he flipped through more pages, he began to understand why there had been no reports, none whatsoever, regarding those two pseudonyms in almost thirteen years. Their call signs had been retired, the only ones in the history of the Deck that had ever done so.

Triad had, of course, placed people within the Deck to gain information on their activities long ago. Those agents had reported back faithfully until they had gone silent at about the same point in time as the disappearance of the Deck's leaders. More agents had been sent into the Deck in an attempt to find out what had happened to the previous undercover operatives and to continue the flow of information, but they had quickly returned, explaining that there had been an overhaul in management and that they could not make entry.

"Are the queen and knave dead?" he mused as he opened another file, "or just retired?" he received his answer in the next file.

Twelve years previously, fleeing from the scene of a rather large theft involving the royal jewels of the ruling house of Zoscar, their crime spree had ended. The Zoscarian defense force chased a ship that was reported to have been carrying the Queen of Diamonds and the Knave of Spades across five systems, firing on them repeatedly, before the ship had been taken down. According to the report, the ship had exploded upon hitting an unusually violent atmosphere.

The jewels had never been recovered and neither had the bodies.

Even more curious than he had been before reading the files, Ryan called Coffee back into his office. "I need whatever information we have on this planet," he said as he handed the report on the Zoscarian jewel theft to his assistant. "What do we know?"

Coffee stepped to another, smaller desk that was tucked into a corner of Commander Moore's sprawling office. He turned on the terminal and began his search. "Class three planet," he explained after just a few moments. "Humanoid inhabitants. Moderate technology levels and no viable space program."

"What's the crime rate like there?" Although Ryan had a sneaking suspicion as to what the answer would be, he wanted to make sure he wasn't reading more into what he saw than what was actually there.

"Pretty standard for that class of planet," Coffee answered after a couple minutes of searching. "But there are a couple of unusual entries you might be interested in."

"What's that?"

"Well," Coffee scanned the terminal as he answered, "About ten years ago, the rate of violent crime started to diminish, particularly relating to violent actions by gangs of any variety, beginning with one of the planet's seven continents and spreading to the other continents as well."

"They have a lot of gang activity there?"

"They did," Coffee agreed. "Now, it has the lowest rate of violent crime in the last fifty years, and nobody seems to know quite why. The drug trade dropped considerably as well, and in about the same time frame, moving from a steady and steep incline of manufacturing and use but lowering. Now it's tapered off almost level.

"This seems to have followed the same pattern of movement through the continents as the other violent crimes did."

"Interesting." Ryan steepled his fingers and tapped them against his chin thoughtfully. "What does that say to you?"

Coffee shrugged. "That someone doesn't like violence and drugs, I guess."

"Can you run a search on that planet's information hubs?"

"Sure," the answer was immediate. "What would you like to know?"

"See if there's any mention of people known as the Queen of Diamonds or the Knave of Spades."

Coffee looked up at him in surprise. "You think they might have been responsible for all this?"

"Maybe. Mostly, I'm just curious. Run the search and see what you find."

For a duo as exceptional in their trade as the thieves known as the Queen of Diamonds and the Knave of Spades had been, it seemed extremely unlikely that they would allow themselves to be taken out of action as easily as the reports indicated. Ryan knew from experience that the easiest way to take the pressure off when someone wanted you either gone or outright dead was to give them exactly what they wanted, even if it meant faking your own death. He had signed off on arrangements for just such an operation for one of his deeply embedded agents just that morning.

Coffee's search didn't take long. Finally, he whistled, low and long. "Found something."

Rather than waiting for the information to be relayed verbally, Ryan stood up and walked across the room, wanting to see for himself.

"Apparently they were rather well-known thieves there," Coffee supplied. "There's even a federal task force dedicated to finding and stopping them." The reports indicated that the pair had been involved in a spree of apparently highly valuable thefts over the last number of years, and it had only been in the last handful that their existence had been recognized. They worked underground, as any master thief would, and were remarkably brazen in their activities, even arranging for sale and delivery of stolen goods to one of that planet's most powerful federal agencies. If these were indeed the same duo who had held the reigns in the Deck, that type of activity was practically child's play.

Ryan walked back over to his desk and settled contentedly into his chair and stacked all of the files neatly on the edge of his desk. When Coffee asked if he wanted the files removed, he shook his head to indicate they should remain. "This," he said thoughtfully as he picked up the pair of playing cards and examined them yet again, "is about to get very interesting."

HOME AWAY FROM HOME AWAY FROM HOME

Diamond and Knave found a good place for their primary base on Majapa, a small planet in the system just beyond the Yareth system. It was warm enough there for them to be comfortable, although not as hot as the tropical paradise Diamond had been looking forward to relocating back on Earth, close enough to Cardiss be able to monitor the Deck's activity and adjust their plans quickly when things changed but far enough away for them to be reasonably safe from attack should any of their plans go horribly wrong.

Because the atmosphere and related surface conditions on Majapa were viable, they didn't have to worry about setting up any artificial life support systems. Even better, there were a handful of residences already built and available for immediate inhabitation. After about a week's worth of examining the available properties and considering how each would fit their needs, the decision was made. The land they selected was comfortable and open-aired, with a courtyard filled with blooming plants in the center of the complex. Diamond fell in love with it the second she saw it.

They found a secondary base as well, in the same system but in a much more obvious location. Ghiel had three moons, one of which had a thriving settlement on it. Because it was located on a moon that didn't have an atmosphere, they had to bring in a construction crew to modify the bare surface enough to make a livable environment. A glassteel bubble, three acres in diameter, was dropped into place, with fifteen landing ports scattered around the perimeter. Most of the buildings inside were standard precast buildings, but they were modular so they could be arranged and expanded as needed. No life bloomed in the garden of dust that surrounded the base, but it didn't matter. This location was far more expensive than the one on Majapa, costing almost the entirety of their remaining credits, but it was absolutely perfect.

Now, they just had to start the revolution.

While the Knave of Spades finalized the purchase and construction of the last of the necessary supplies for both of their new bases, Diamond called Protus. She had stalled on that particular task as long as she possibly could, but time had finally run out. They had scheduled a meeting with their new team in less than a week and without the psionist's input, they wouldn't know which of them could be trusted and which were spies.

"I was wondering how long it would be before you'd call," he said as he answered.

"You know who this is?" The question was rhetorical; of course, he knew. Diamond just hated it when he said things like that, and Protus knew it. As a psionist, he could read the minds of people at almost any time he chose, so he could easily determine who was on the other end of the comm and decide whether or not to answer it based on that knowledge. On more than one occasion, he had decided against accepting Diamond's call because he had either been uninterested in her request or had been busy elsewhere and would not be available for assistance. Hesitant as she had been about contacting him, she was just glad he accepted her call. She and Knave didn't have much of a backup idea for this part of the plan, so if he hadn't answered, or if he refused their request, they were stuck and would have to reconsider their entire operation.

"Of course, I know," he drawled, echoing her thoughts perfectly. "And I'm happier than a flying flamingo to hear from you. Once I discovered you were back in the area, I knew it was only a matter of time before I heard your sweet voice again. I just wish it was under better circumstances. You know, you can call occasionally just to say hello, it doesn't always have to be because you need my help. I'm always here for you."

"That's great. I..."

"You know," he interrupted her. "I almost started to believe all those rumors about you being dead, giving what's been going on with the Deck lately. I know you wouldn't have ever put up with that kind of garbage using your good name for bad."

She could almost *hear* him grinning on the other end of the comm and she gritted her teeth in response. Being constantly interrupted was one of her personal pet peeves and while he normally only did so a couple of times during each of their conversations, he was apparently making up for lost time. The barely veiled flirting wasn't helpful for her mood either, as they both knew she had no interest in him. "Look, I..."

"I understand," he said before she could finish. "None of this is what you had wanted, nor are you responsible for any of it, as I'm sure you already know. You couldn't help being stuck. It was a terrible situation, I'm sure, but at least you made the best of it. I'm just surprised it took you so long to find your way back. But yes, now that you've returned, it's time to clean house."

"Exactly. Could..."

Again, he interrupted her. "Of course, I'll come out to meet with your minions. Safety first, and all that. I have already cleared my schedule for the next couple of weeks and I can clear out more if necessary, so rest assured that you will have my complete and undivided attention for as long as you need me."

She gritted her teeth in consternation. As if his mind-reading wasn't annoying enough, his constant habit of interruption was infuriating. "They aren't minions," she said. Her *tress* began to show her irritation as faint lines started appearing beneath her skin.

"Of course not," he drawled in amused, condescending tone. "I'll start heading towards your system in the morning. Are we all meeting on Ghiel or on Majapa?"

She shouldn't have been surprised that he knew about their activities, but it was still unnerving. "Can you meet us on the lunar base?" she asked through tightly-clenched teeth, "or do we need to..."

"Naw, I can get there on my own. I have a couple of friends who owe me a favor and they're heading out in that direction anyway. See you in a few days, then." He cut the line immediately, so as Diamond switched off her comm, she was seething even more than before. Not only had he been interrupting her for the entire conversation, if it could even really be called a conversation, now he had hung up on her.

"Nice talking to you, too," she grumbled under her breath, wondering when the infuriating man had found someone daft enough to call him a friend. As she calmed, however, she realized that he probably had plenty of friends scattered around the galaxy, herself included. Just because a friendship wasn't traditional, that didn't mean it didn't exist.

One of the primary reasons why the used Protus as often as they did, despite the frustration she felt every time she had to make contact with him, was because the man was quite good.

Where almost every other time Diamond had encountered a psionist, she had been able to tell when her mind was being probed. It always caused a soft pressure sensation in her head; from her research she had discovered that was the most common trait of a mental invasion. With Protus, on the other hand, there was no pressure, no sensations of being mentally scanned at all. In fact, if he didn't regularly show her that he knew exactly what she was thinking, she would almost begin to wonder if he had any psionic abilities at all.

The first few times she had been in contact with him, she had been extremely wary. While everyone had secrets, as she well knew, hers were unique and she wasn't excited about the idea of someone having the ability to know everything going on in her mind at any time they wanted. She and Protus had come to an agreement long ago that he would respect her privacy and would only read her surface thoughts unless she invited him deeper, which she didn't see a time where she would ever be inclined, or it became unavoidable.

Plus, she knew the man was absolutely trustworthy, which he had proven on more occasions than she could count.

She sent Knave a thumbs-up. It was a strange custom from the planet where they had just spent more than a decade, which meant that everything was good. Both of them had gotten into the habit of using it when signaling to each other. In their current environment, using some of the gestures from Earth suited their needs even more, as nobody around them could possibly know what some of their newly-discovered signals meant.

As soon as he finished his business at the bank, it was time to head back toward the lunar base on Ghiel to call in the troops.

DISHONOR AMONG THIEVES

The King of Clubs was not in a good mood. Up until that morning, everything had been going so well, but now someone had to go and ruin it. He glared across the breakfast table at the Ace of Diamonds, one of the few people brave enough to get him out of bed before his usual time to rise.

And he had yet to explain why.

The King of Clubs was a human, originally from one of the outposts in the Tyrannus system. Although he was just a couple tenths less than two units tall, he wore boots with heels that lifted him almost five tenths, simply to appear more imposing. His eyes were a cold, emotionless blue beneath a dark brown tangle of hair that fell, when combed, in waves almost to his waist. Because he had been roused from his bed for a matter of urgent attention, he hadn't bothered to do more than throw on the nearest available clothing before meeting the Ace in the dining hall. As a result, he was dressed in wrinkled black trousers left over from the previous day, a black short-sleeved undershirt, and his favorite boots.

A young servant girl, one of the spoils the King had personally selected from the takeover of the Xerxes system, brought a pair of steaming plates and set them down before the two men, neither of whom looked up or gave any acknowledgement of either the food's arrival or the servant's presence.

"There are two problems requiring your attention, your highness," the Ace finally spoke after the room was empty but for the two of them. "First of all, there has been an increase in movement in the Vergling territories. Something has stirred them up, and they have renewed and strengthened their defenses."

The Ace of Diamonds was human as well, or at least he appeared to be so, dark of both skin and hair. His eyes, on the other hand, were a pale shade of blue that looked silvery-white in the dim morning light. He was dressed in all black, the standard uniform of the Deck, but unlike the rest of the cards, he wore no insignia that announced his rank. The only identifying marks he wore were the twin golden diamond-shaped crystals set into his lapels.

"How bad?" the King asked as he reached for his silverware.

"Half of your force has been driven back already."

He grunted in response. The Verglings controlled a large section of the Oberron system, which had a disgustingly large amount of Myrite, one of the most efficient, and therefore most expensive, fuel chemicals in the galaxy. The King of Clubs had begun moving troops to take over their supply lines almost two years ago and, frustratingly, had not yet managed to gain a solid foothold in Vergling territory.

Because of that, the Ace's news was a fairly major setback, as it meant months of work had just been annihilated. King scowled and stabbed at his food. The force that had just been thwarted was the most powerful assault that the Deck had launched into that zone yet. Their loss was a substantial defeat, one he didn't intend to leave unpunished. The Verglings would pay for the insult, as would any of the troops who dared return home.

As important as the information undoubtedly was, it still didn't warrant bringing him out of bed an hour early. "Send in a force of Aces," he ordered between bites. "Send them behind the Vergling lines to weaken their defense." The King's distaste for Verglings, small insect-like beings that he fully believed should be exterminated in their entirety, was well-known. "If your people are as good as they're supposed to be, you might even be able to take out some of their hierarchy and they'll stop putting up so much resistance." He chewed slowly and continued. "How much of their defense did we remove before retreating?"

"Not much," the Ace admitted. "Their defenses were already increasing before we arrived. It's almost as though they were expecting us."

"How could they have been expecting us?" the King demanded. "This maneuver was supposed to be kept secret. Only myself and a handful of your own men knew what we were planning. So how did they know we were coming?"

"We suspect that they simply realized we were intent on our assault." The answer was simple and obvious. The Deck had been assaulting the Oberron system for years, increasing their forces each time they had to regroup. Additional troops and tactics sent in that direction could hardly be considered a surprise.

"Is that all, your highness?" He wasn't positive, but the tone of the Ace's voice sounded almost condescending.

"Of course not, you fool," the King snapped. "Send in more troops to bolster the offensive line. Do we have contacts left in World Industries?"

World Industries was one of the galaxy's leading manufacturers of spaceships and weaponry. Most of their products were military only, designated for Triad's exclusive use until the models became outdated enough for others to purchase. A handful of years previously, the Deck had managed to place a handful of people into key positions within their purchasing and acquisitions departments in order to get military technology and weapons for their own use, well ahead of any other non-military group in existence. When the Ace agreed that they still had people in place, he continued. "Order more ships, the best stuff they've got. I don't care how much it costs, just do it. Load them up with weapons, long range stuff, and kill off those pests already."

"Once the Aces have done their jobs," he stabbed another bite of food, "ground troops can move in again and finish the cleanup. I expect to hear that we have the Myrite supply lines in our grasp shortly."

"Very well, sir." The Ace took a small bite from his own plate, trying to keep his distaste from showing on his expression. The food was unusual, and he wasn't even sure which planet it had come from, let alone what it was. The King of Clubs prided himself on having the most exotic foods at every meal, and if the Ace didn't at least make an attempt at consuming it, he would become offended. He would be even more offended if he believed that his guests, willingly or otherwise, weren't enjoying it.

"I assume you have more." The King's steely blue eyes looked unblinkingly at him from across the table. "You did, after all, start by saying there were *two* problems seeking my immediate attention." He smiled, coldly and without mirth. "But you have spoken only of one."

"That is true, your highness." The Ace took another small bite before continuing. "I wanted to give you the opportunity to fully wake before startling you with the second piece of business."

"I am fully awake," the King huffed, "so get on with it."

"Very well. My office received a message late last night. This message indicated that there is a resistance force among the ranks, a group who are attempting to call for a massive, Deck-wide revolt."

The King grunted without looking up from his plate. When he had first taken over the Deck, there had been many challenges to his authority, but the Aces had ensured his continued leadership. As a result, there hadn't been any substantial resistance in over five years. "Not the first of those we've heard of and unlikely to be the last. This news is hardly startling."

"Under normal circumstances, that would be true," the Ace agreed.

"Just kill them and be done with it." His response was no surprise, his automatic orders for any hints of revolt was death to the traitors. This had already led to a widespread shuffling of the cards throughout the ranks as the highest levels of cards, particularly face cards, had been systematically eliminated. Any who remained loyal to his predecessor, either in fact or merely by suspicion, were removed before they could undermine his authority. His rule was absolute, he had seen to it personally.

"This is different from resistances you have defeated in the past," the Ace continued as though the King hadn't spoken at all. "Someone is passing the rumor that the Queen of Diamonds and Knave of Spades have returned."

That got his attention. The King of Clubs's head shot up, his eyes narrowed in malice. "Nonsense. If they were still alive, someone would have heard about it years ago." He shook his head. "How many people have heard about this?"

"I cannot say for certain," the Ace responded. "As I understand, everyone who was a part of the Deck twelve years ago, and who is raked at less than an Eight, is being contacted."

This was no small news. Even if it wasn't true, just the circulating rumor that the previous leaders of the Deck had returned could put a substantial hitch into all of the King's plans. Although he had made clear that his rule was absolute, there were likely to be plenty of people yet among his ranks who still held a small spark of loyalty to their long-dead leaders.

Even worse, he realized, if someone was actually claiming to be the Queen of Diamonds and the Knave of Spades, miraculously returned from the dead, he would have a big problem on his hands. The imposters needed to be found quickly and dealt with before they could do any more damage than what had already been done.

"Fine," the King snapped. "Find out where this rumor started and kill them." He scraped his fork loudly against the plate as he scooped up another bite and shoveled it into his mouth. "And whoever's spreading it, kill them, too."

"Of course, your highness." The Ace turned from his seat, as if preparing to leave. Before standing, however, he turned to look at the King. "If I could make a suggestion before I leave, though."

"What's that?"

"Well, it occurs to me that this might be an excellent opportunity," he said as he settled back into his seat.

"An opportunity for what, exactly?"

"As I'm sure you understand, finding those responsible for this rumor would be time-consuming and take a large force of our people away from much more important tasks."

The King grunted but motioned for him to continue.

"Why don't we send some of your trusted people, perhaps even a small contingent of Aces, to find out exactly what's going on and to report back?

"Right now, there isn't a lot of information passing along the lines, so if we can get someone in the inside, they can find out what the resistance is all about. You know," he looked slyly across the table, "information about who is in charge of it, what their intentions are, that type of thing. Information that would be useful for you to ensure this nasty business is thoroughly eradicated."

The King of Clubs thought over his words. "Once we have that," he conceded, "we can move and be a lot more efficient than if we struck right now."

"Exactly, your highness," the Ace agreed. "Why, it would be premature to act now, without all of the information, and may even strengthen the resistance."

It didn't take much more for the King of Clubs to see things from the Ace of Diamonds's point of view, as usual. The Ace smiled, took one last bite of the horrendous food that the King's cooks had made for them, and headed out to select people to send into the traitors' den.

MEETING OF THE MINDS

Diamond and Knave had expected to have a reasonable number of attendees at their meeting, but they had been completely unprepared for the sheer quantity of people who had responded to their call. There were some people they recognized from before their exile, but those were few and far between in the crowd of people. So many, in fact, had responded to their call that they couldn't all fit into the meeting space that the pair had reserved for the evening.

Protus had showed up, ahead of schedule as expected. He was dressed in his usual style of a flowing white linen tunic that fell to just below his knees and a pair of equally billowy trousers. The lightness of the fabric only accentuated the darkness of his skin, which was only barely lighter than the void of space outside and covered in raised brands, scars on every visible surface of his body that indicated the brutal way his people enacted to coerce information from any of their psionists who refused to divulge it willingly. The visible skin wasn't the only place where he was marked, they both knew. His face and hands were simply examples of the damage that covered his body.

In all of the other survivors of such methods Diamond had ever seen, none of them had more than the barest minimal of scars to show what they had been through; in almost every case each had capitulated before the damage became so extensive. Protus, on the other hand, had never been coerced into handing over a single piece of confidential information. He wore the brands on his skin as a badge of honor, a testament to the price he had been willing to pay for his silence and the trust that had been placed within his secrets.

That level of damage was, in fact, one of the reasons that Knave and Diamond trusted him so implicitly. Though he aggravated Diamond every time she had to deal with him, she couldn't deny his track record. If anyone was going to be honest with them, Protus was it.

The Four of Hearts brought her cadre as well. None of them looked as nervous as they had appeared the first time meeting on the base but there was still a heightened awareness around them, a sense that they knew that they would all be brutally put to death if their actions were discovered. Not by Knave and Diamond, of course, but by the so-called King of Clubs, the man who had usurped and perverted their precious Deck. Given the heavy hand under which they had been living for the past many years, they could be forgiven for not realizing that they were safe in the hands of their true leaders.

Partly because she had already met with them and partly to help alleviate everyone's fears, Diamond called Four and her group to speak with her and Protus first.

She had already met all of the members of that particular group, but whether it was because of the distressing news that they were discussing or because she hadn't been paying close enough attention, most of the details about who they were and what they looked like had faded almost immediately. In the past, Diamond hadn't felt the need to know all of the people she was working with, as only those with whom she worked with regularly required her specific attention, but recent events had caused her to rethink her judgment. Maintaining a good relationship with her crew couldn't hurt, and as she was about to prove to the usurper, the lowest ranking members of any organization were the foundation upon which the entire Deck stood. Without them and the sturdy base they provided, nothing could stand.

She wasn't as worried about remembering everyone's suit and rank, as it seemed that the suits they had been given seemed arbitrary at best and Diamond had no intention of letting her cards' ranks stay in the mess they were in.

The four suits were an easy way to classify which type of card each person was and where each of their strengths lay. Hearts were easily the flashiest, often relying on charm and charisma to get what they want and as such were regularly used to open new avenues of business by generating relationships with those in power and tactfully questioning those around them to glean necessary information. Diamonds were the sneakiest of the bunch, able to get into and out of secure areas with as little trace as possible and were used to break into secure areas, either to retrieve information and valuables or to plant misleading information. Spades were intelligent, able to gather and process information quickly, so while they didn't often work in the field, each group sent out on mission had at least one Spade in place to monitor activity and ensure the safety and success of the team. Clubs were the brutes, those who had enough strength or firepower to back them up in any situation and were commonly used for base defense and to send into situations that were particularly dangerous when there was a chance of combat. At first, Diamond had been hesitant about the use of Clubs and had kept very few of them in the Deck, but over time, she had come to appreciate the value of their assignments.

She identified the Four of Hearts immediately. Her enormous eyes were bright turquoise and her pale brown hair was piled on top of her head in an intricate mass of braids. Diamond introduced the woman to Protus and let the pair of them talk for a moment while she committed the rest of her team to memory.

Three of the four humans in Four's group were men. Of them, the first was short and slender with solemn brown eyes the color of honey and hair to match. He didn't smile as Diamond took his hand in greeting, barely looking up to meet her eyes. Whether his refusal to meet her gaze was the result of shyness or shame, she wasn't sure. That's what Protus was there to discover.

Spade, she mused to herself as she evaluated him, *or Diamond.* The small man wasn't flashy enough to be a Heart, nor did he seem aggressive enough to be a Club. His size was perfect for the work of a diamond, but his demeanor could easily hide plenty of promise in just about any suit except clubs, if she wasn't mistaken.

The next man was taller, with tightly corded muscle. He had jet black hair and deep brown eyes that sparkled with amusement. He had been grinning when Diamond had spotted them from across the room, and his smile hadn't faltered.

Now that's a Heart, she found herself grinning in return. While his muscle indicated his ability to be a club, his charisma alone indicated his strength in the hearts suit.

The third male human in the group was about the same height as the first man, with pale blond hair and hazel eyes which never seemed to stop moving. He glanced at her a few times while she was meeting the rest of the group before focusing on other people in the area, his own group and Protus included. His glances didn't seem to be threatening as much as wary and Diamond had to wonder whether he was looking for someone or something in particular or whether he was just as nervous as the rest of the people around him.

Spade, she decided. No matter what he was looking for, he was far more aware of his surroundings than most of the rest of the people in the room and was likely already planning escape routes should things go wrong.

The female human was barely larger than the first man Diamond had evaluated. Her hair was a beautiful shade of deep chestnut brown that reflected red in the lights of the meeting room and her blue eyes were flecked with green. Rather than refusing to meet her eyes, however, the woman reached out to take her hand at the same moment she moved to offer it.

Not flashy enough to be a Heart, Diamond thought, *but probably not a Diamond either.* A lifetime of training taught her what to look for, and she was able to detect a hint of the woman's fighting skill beneath the surface. *Club*, she decided. *Definitely a Club.*

The Tet was already assigned to the ranks of the Clubs, which was fitting given his race's natural inclination towards battle and all things combat related. She decided to let that stand. The Dolrathi, on the other hand, had been assigned to the Hearts.

"What were they thinking?" She muttered to herself as she moved on to the next group. "They're no more a Heart than the Tet is." The Dolrathi would be far more effective as a Spade. With their powers of observation, as long as they had the analytical skills to match, they could become a valuable asset instead of withering among the ranks of a group that they didn't belong in. While it wasn't impossible for a Dolrathi to be a heart, it would have to be a truly exceptional Dolrathi.

Knave was nowhere near Diamond while she was meeting the new members of their crew. Instead, he stayed near the back of the room to evaluate everyone, both the interactions of the ones who were talking with Protus and Diamond and the ones who had either not yet had the opportunity to meet them or who had already gone through the process and were waiting for sorting and further orders.

He was quite good at reading body language, as all Spades *should* be, so just by watching, he was able to determine a rough estimate of which people would be able to work well together and who would easily be able to blend from one group to another.

Finally, this arrangement allowed Protus to psionically examine each attendee to determine who could be trusted and who had been sent there to spy on their activities. After talking with over a hundred and fifty people, only fourteen of them caused him to frown.

To Diamond's dismay, one of those was the human woman that Four had brought to their first meeting.

Once all of the attendees had been personally welcomed to the group by the Queen of Diamonds and Protus, Knave began to divide them into two groups. "You guys will be going to Ghiel to set up and maintain our main base," he explained to them as he led them out of the room. "This base will be our primary point of all activities from here on out. It will also be where we make and maintain all of our plans."

All of the people Protus had indicated as untrustworthy were placed in the Ghiel team, as well as the Four of Hearts and all of the people she had brought with her. About a dozen other people were arbitrarily selected to belong to the group as well.

As soon as Knave and his people were out of the door and out of hearing distance, Diamond gathered the rest of the group and led them out as well. "You are being sent to Majapa," she explained as she led them down the narrow corridor. "We have a new base there that should be just about finished getting set up by the time you arrive. All you guys need to do for right now is to settle in and wait for further instructions."

"Ma'am?" One person called out from the middle of the group.

Although Diamond turned around as soon as the voice had spoken, there were simply too many people crowded into the area to identify from whom it had come. "Yes?"

"Will we be able to contact any of the other bases?" the voice called out. "Or you?"

"You will have a way to communicate with myself and Knave," she reassured them. "There will be no contact between your base and the other bases at this time."

"Why?" A different voice called out.

"All will be explained in due time. But for right now, we need to make sure that communications are going where, and only where, we need them to.

"Communications between bases will open as soon as possible. But for right now, we just can't take that chance."

"Do you think one of us is a spy?"

She stopped in front of the airlock that would lead them to their waiting ships and turned back to face her followers. "No. We know that none of you are spies. Contact among everyone on all of our bases is limited to those on the base with you and Knave and me. We will be moving between the bases, so there will be plenty of opportunity for the sending and receiving of messages to and from people on other bases.

"But for now, we need to begin setting the next phase of the plan into motion and that requires absolute silence." With that, she herded everyone onto the waiting ship, answering no further questions, and waited to see it leave before heading back to meet up with Knave.

Diamond and Knave spent three days on their own ship, slowly drifting through the system so that they were always moving and remained well out of eavesdropping range, going over all of the information they had gathered from the meeting and comparing notes.

"First things first, we need a better hierarchy, and that means we need to promote someone to face," she explained to Knave. "Someone has to be able to maintain order and I don't want to have to hand orders to twenty different people every time I need to get something done."

He agreed without argument. "What about him?" he tapped on one of her notes. "He seems like he'd be capable."

She shook her head. "Not self-assured enough." She pulled another paper on top of the stack. "I was thinking maybe him."

"Bad idea. He'll bully the people below him."

"Really?" She looked at her notes more closely. "But I thought he'd be a good Heart, not a Club."

"I didn't say he'd be a Club," he agreed with her. "But fighting isn't the only way to be a bully."

She pondered the thought for a while, finally conceding his point. "Okay, so what do we think about this one?"

He looked at it for a long moment before turning the page so that he wouldn't have to continue reading it upside down. "It has some appeal," he finally agreed.

The young man she was looking at was a human, not surprising because humans were the most common race to be found. He wasn't just agreeing because he was a Spade, either, she knew. Knave wasn't petty like that. Although the man was currently ranked among the diamonds, they both knew that he would be reassigned as a Spade.

"He was talking to a few different groups of people at the meeting," he explained, "and a lot of people who weren't already in groups." His forehead creased into a frown. "I'm surprised I didn't think of him."

"Nobody's perfect," she chuckled as she set the paper aside. "Not even you."

They decided to make the newly-assigned Spade a Ten and selected four other people to promote to Nines of all four suits.

With the combined efforts of those five people, they were sure the remaining cards could be shuffled into place.

Diamond and Knave traveled to Majapa first. Not for any ranking or hierarchy, or even because it was the place they knew had not yet been infiltrated. Simply enough, it was closer.

Their cards had barely been able to settle in during the three days they had been stationed there and Diamond wanted to set a ranking order before any in-fighting had a chance to begin. The last thing she needed was an upstart wanting to make a power play and damaging the fresh cards before anything had been done with them.

When they landed on Majapa, they began to search for their selected people. The Ten of Spades was easy to spot; at over two units tall, much taller than the average human, he would be hard to *not* be spotted. He brushed his short brown hair away from his face as he caught them striding towards him and jogged to meet them halfway, smiling nervously.

A large crowd had gathered around Knave and Diamond as they had walked through the base, so there were plenty of witnesses to her first proclamation. "You are no longer a Diamond," she said as she stopped before him. "As of this moment, you are a Spade."

He blinked at her in surprise. "Um," he said as he searched for words, looking between her and Knave cautiously. "Okay."

"Furthermore," she said without letting him stammer, "you are promoted to the rank of Ten and are in control of this base until further notice."

He gaped at her in outright shock. "Are you serious?" he asked, his voice breathless.

"Of course, I'm sure." She handed him a handful of papers. "These people need their suits changed as well, make sure that happens before my next visit."

He blinked at her for a few times, visibly shook himself, and glanced at the papers. "Yeah, I mean, no problem."

Knave stepped forward with a male Emovete in tow. The Emovete had hair that was so black it shined blue in the light and hung perfectly straight down his back almost to his waist.

"You are also now a Spade," she explained to the newcomer, "and promoted to the rank of Nine."

Knave brought forth three more people: a human female with unnaturally dyed red hair that hung in thick waves to the middle of her back, a human male with close-cropped brown hair and blue eyes, and a second human female with blond hair and blue eyes. These, Diamond introduced as Nines of Hearts, Diamonds, and Clubs, respectively.

"As I said," Diamond turned back to the Ten, "You will have the rest of the people on your base re-suited before my return. Furthermore, you will determine a ranking structure among them." She let her glance fall to the Nines as well. "This responsibility lies with all of you, and I expect you to work with each other, not against. Is that understood?"

All of them vigorously nodded their agreement, so she turned back to the Ten. "There are a couple more things I want you to get started on." She handed him another stack of papers. "These people were personal contacts of mine and Knave's. Someone needs to open communication with all of them and let them know we're back in business."

Because the list she handed over had never been public knowledge, even among members of the Deck, Diamond was reasonably certain that these specific contacts had not been tampered with. At least, she hoped they hadn't, but she realized a lot could happen in thirteen years.

"Also, I want you searching around the next system out to see what is available and what can be obtained with relative safety." They weren't interested in losing any of their members so quickly after getting them back into the fold, so Knave and Diamond had agreed that, at least for the first while, none of their fresh cards would be sent out on anything dangerous.

"When I return," she added as she turned to leave, "I want a full report."

Done there, she and Knave headed to Ghiel. There had been almost as much discussion about who would be placed in charge at Ghiel as there had been at Majapa.

"I want to put Four in charge," Diamond had pointed out during the discussion, "but I don't think I'm going to."

"Why not?" Knave looked at her in surprise. "Protus cleared her, so we know she can be trusted. She's perfect."

"I know," she sighed in frustration. "But if there are any attempts to seize control, I don't want to put her in danger."

He looked at the papers thoughtfully. "I don't think that's so much of an *if* as a *when*."

"Exactly. While she may be good to lead, I don't want to make her a lieutenant quite yet."

"But that also means that no matter who we put in charge, someone's going to have to deal with an uprising."

"That's why I'm thinking about promoting him," she pushed a paper in front of him, "to be a Ten."

He let out a low whistle as he picked up the paper, recognizing her logic immediately. Really, there was only one problem he could foresee. "How do you think they'll react to having a Club in charge?"

"Doesn't matter," she smiled faintly. "There are only four suits, so eventually they're going to have to get used to having another Club in charge."

After a bit more discussion, he agreed. The four recruits who would be placed as Nines were unusual choices as well, but she was adamant. "These are the ones it has to be," she stressed.

"But you're deliberately putting a traitor in charge."

"No," she shook her head, "I'm deliberately putting a traitor into perfect position for the Ten to keep an eye on."

"And what about the rest of the traitors?"

"We'll take care of them later. With any luck, our new Ten will realize there's a problem and take care of it for us." She wasn't optimistic about the last happening, but it was a nice idea.

There was no point in wandering through the throngs of people on Ghiel as they had done on Majapa. There were far fewer people there, so it was much easier to just call a meeting.

The first person that Diamond called forward was the Tet, originally a member of Four's group. "You were well assigned a Club," She said when he stepped forward. "You have been promoted to Ten. Congratulations, you are now in charge of this base."

She ignored the gasps of surprise from the congregated group, instead turning to search for the rest of her selections.

Four was easy enough to locate. She stood in the front line of witnesses, a wide grin of pride at the promotion of her friend, tinged with a hint of jealousy. "Four," Diamond called her forward as well.

The pride and jealousy turned to surprise as the Emovete stepped forward.

"You are now advanced to Nine and will assist Ten in the operations of this base."

The newly-appointed Nine's eyes widened, looking for all appearances that they were about to encompass the entire top half of her head. "Thank you," she breathed, almost inaudibly beneath the shouts of the crowd behind her. Her *tress* flickered in pride.

All of the promotions Diamond gave that day involved members of the Emovete's original group. The Dolrathi was moved from the suit of Hearts to Spades and promoted to Nine. The young man with honey-colored hair who had refused eye contact was promoted as well and set as a Diamond. He looked up in shock at the promotion, and Diamond discovered that his eyes were slightly darker than the honey color she had originally thought.

Finally, the auburn-haired woman was placed as the Nine of Clubs. Diamond wasn't sure if she saw a glint of satisfaction in the woman's green-flecked eyes, but it didn't matter. She knew that the woman was a traitor, but she also knew that if the woman staged a revolt, she would have to stand against the Tet. A lifetime had taught the Queen of Diamonds how to evaluate an opponent's fighting skill, and she had no doubts about which of them would be overmatched in that battle.

As she had on Majapa, she gave the Ten a list of people who needed to have their suits changed and told the five officers to arrange the rest of the staff as they saw fit.

The list of potential contacts that she handed over to the Ghiel cards was much longer than the list they had given to the Majapans, despite their smaller membership. While all of the contacts on the second list were every bit as viable as the first ones had been, they were also contacts that most of the Deck had known about.

This was intentional. Any information the Ghiel cards got from that list and sent back to the King of Clubs would be useless, at best.

Also, as on Majapa, the Ghiel cards were instructed to investigate their area to look for acquisitions. "Be careful," Diamond cautioned them as she made her way back towards her waiting ship. "We don't want to put anyone into any more danger than necessary."

After promising to return for reports, she followed Knave onto their waiting ship.

ENEMY OF MY ENEMY

"What's the next phase of the plan?" Knave looked up from his console to meet Diamond's eyes. "Now that you've got your bases up and running, I'm sure you're already working on the next part."

She giggled and turned back to her own console. "Sometimes," she said, "I think you might know me too well."

"Does that mean you've got a plan?"

"Well, it's not a plan, per se, but more of a plan to make a plan."

He blinked at her in silence for a moment. "You're serious," he decided. "Okay, so what's the plan to make a plan?"

"The first step, of course, is to get funds flowing again. With both groups looking for viable opportunities, the bases should be able to start showing some progress on that soon. Once that's going, we've got two options. We can either start chipping away at the King's Deck or we can start dismantling his Roxxy distribution chain."

"If I recall correctly, it's only the people loyal to the King who have information about their distribution, so it seems like those can both be done simultaneously."

She nodded her agreement with his logic. "By taking out his supply chain and the people who are managing it, that will put a dent in his income, his people, and take at least some of the drug out of the picture." She had no illusions about being able to take Roxxy off the market completely; they hadn't even been able to do that on the single planet they had recently lived on.

"Ah," Knave nodded slowly in comprehension. "And that's where you're stuck."

It was true. Because of Diamond's resistance to violence, killing any cards who were loyal to the King was out of the question. "I'm trying to figure out how to take his people away from him," she said. "I've been wracking my brain, but everything lately seems to lead back to violence and killing people." She looked up at her friend, her green eyes sad. "And I can't do that anymore."

Both of them sat in silence, thinking, for the next hour and a half, until Knave's head snapped up and turned to Diamond. "Why don't we do it the same way we did back on Earth?"

Diamond chuckled. "You really think deVann and his task force can manage all these people?" she asked. "Heck, he couldn't even manage *us.*"

"No," He shook his head. "I'm not thinking deVann. I'm not even thinking the FBI."

"Good," she muttered. "A well-trained human would tear them apart." She shuddered. "I'd hate to think of what would happen if we handed them a Tet." Earthlings had no notion of what a Tet was, let alone what one was capable of. Since they weren't a space-travelling civilization yet, even though they badly wanted to be one, the people of Earth were still convinced that their species was the only one in the universe. She and Knave had spent months laughing at that idea once they discovered how stunted their new neighbors' knowledge of their place in the galaxy truly was.

He shook his head again. "We were stuck on that little planet too long. We started thinking like Earthlings."

Her eyes narrowed as he spoke. "What's that supposed to mean?"

"It means, I mention an organization designed to capture and contain criminals, and you automatically jumped to the FBI."

"No, you didn't," she protested, "You were talking about what we did on Earth. That was what we did on Earth."

"But we're not on Earth anymore," he said, "and even back there, the FBI wasn't the only group we assisted. Have you forgotten about the DEA?" The DEA was the drug enforcement agency, with whom Knave and Diamond had worked closely, if unwittingly on the DEA's part, to minimize the drug traffic on the planet. "Out among the stars, there are completely different powers at play."

Her eyes opened back to their natural position as comprehension set in. "No," she denied. "I can't do that."

"You're the only one who can," he said gently. "You've already opened a dialogue with them. And if we're going to do this without killing anyone, they're the only ones who can contain them."

They argued for another hour, with Diamond losing ground with every minute that passed. Finally, she had to fold her hand. "Fine," she grumbled. "Not that I think they'll be eager to help us, but I'll see what I can do."

"Of course they'll help," Knave leaned comfortably back in his seat, secure in his victory. "Remember the news feeds? They've already been tasked with taking out the problem with the Deck. We'll just be helping them along a little bit. And it's the King's own fault: he's the one that put them on the wanted list."

"And us, too, in case you've forgotten."

Diamond hated the idea of contacting Triad. She had spent almost her entire life trying to stay under their radar, or at least nonthreatening enough to make them not care enough to pay attention. But Knave was right. The only way that they could keep the King's cards out of the way would be with their help.

She didn't want to get involved with any portion of the Interplanetary Government, let alone their military, but her own words came back to haunt her. She was involved, whether she wanted to be or not.

Besides, she reasoned, if she somehow could, by some miracle, come to an arrangement with Commander Moore, she might be able to keep Triad's armies from coming after her newly assembled Deck.

Including herself and Knave.

Finding Triad was the easy part. The military was based on Lovus, a planet that wasn't very far away as far as galaxies were concerned. Diamond had always wanted to see Lovus; everything she had heard about Triad's ring-encircled home world said that it was breathtakingly beautiful, one of the cleanest inhabited planets anywhere.

Wanting to go and actually going were two very different things, however. She had been afraid to set foot on any planet that was teeming with military, psionists, and some of the finest examples of battle craft known to the galaxy. Most of the Interplanetary Government's ships were built by World Industries, a Lovus-based company, and even the StarrTech computers that she used on a daily basis were of Lovan manufacture.

Lovan manufacture, she thought to herself, *that's a laugh.* StarrTech was a subsidiary of Starr Enterprises, owned by one of the most famous, most lethal, and most feared of all Triad's soldiers. Nobody knew her real name, just as nobody knew Diamond's, but the person called Gazer had been hand-selected by Triad's headhunters for her skills in strategy, biotechnologies, and infiltration. Diamond would just about kill to have someone with her skills in her Deck.

To have someone like that hunting her Deck was an absolute nightmare.

Not to mention her psionic abilities. Gazer's mental powers made Protus look like a baby still in diapers in comparison. Of all the people in Triad, Gazer was the one person the Queen of Diamonds feared the most. She was the sole reason, no matter what excuses she made to everyone else, that Diamond had never been brave enough to set foot on Lovan soil.

If they could just get a decent working relationship with Triad, she just might be able to see it before she died, even if only once.

Nervous but determined, trying to push the nightmarish thoughts of Gazer from her mind, she picked up her phone and began to dial.

Someone had to have Commander Moore's office number.

MOUTH OF THE LION

It never failed, Ryan grumbled to himself. Every day, just as he was about to go home, someone would either show up or call in with something important. "Or rather," he said as he settled back into his chair, "something they think is important."

Coffee had called him over the intercom just as he had shut his computer off and stood to leave. "Commander Moore," he called, "you have an incoming comm."

"They can leave a message," he responded. "I've left for the day."

"I would, but this person claims to be the Queen of Diamonds."

Surprised, Ryan snapped to attention and looked at the pair of playing cards that still sat on his desk. The fruits that had been included in the basket had long since been devoured as a series of midafternoon snacks and a missed lunch, but he had insisted that the cards remain where he had put them.

He started the tracing program on his comm unit, even knowing that there were likely other programs, clones of the one he used, already in process. Coffee would have started his, at the very least. Still, Ryan had been the one to put the regulations in place which demanded that all possible threats had to be dealt with in the same manner. Although his gut instinct told him that this phone call wasn't a threat, he still had to set the example.

After all, if even he wouldn't follow his regulations, how could he expect anyone else to follow them?

Once he received the signal that the trace had begun its work, he picked up his phone. "This is Commander Moore."

"Commander," a low, feminine voice purred into his ear. "So nice to be speaking directly to you at last."

"I would say the same," he answered levelly, "but I'm not entirely convinced of whom I am speaking with."

"Did you receive the basket?" the voice asked without hesitation.

"Yes," he admitted. "It was a bit of a surprise, I admit. I hadn't expected to receive one, considering that the reports I have say you're dead."

"Reports can be deceiving," she breathed. "I hope you liked the star-fruit. It's a personal favorite of mine."

"I did," he admitted honestly. The star-shaped fruits had confused him at first and he had been leery of tasting them, but they had been smooth and citrusy, without being overpowering. "You must tell me where those came from. My aides wanted to sample them as well, but there were only two, and those were rather small."

"I'll be sure to send you some more," she promised.

As appealing as her offer was, Ryan doubted that she had called simply to discuss the fruits. "So," he changed the subject, "if my reports of your death are wrong, where have you been? Nobody's heard from you in well over ten years."

"I was stranded on a planet," she pouted. "One that wasn't even space capable. It took far too long to find a way back off of it, and then I found out what a mess had been made of my Deck while I was gone."

"Yes," he agreed. "As I understand it, things took a rather drastic turn for the worse without you."

"Unfortunately," she sighed, "that is true. I want to reassure you that I have already begun my efforts to clean up this particular mess and I would hope that you and your people would be willing to give me and mine enough time and space to work."

Finally, he thought, the crux of the matter. He had no doubt that he was speaking to the true Queen of Diamonds, although it was still surprising that she had contacted him directly. For all of the years that she and her Deck had been in business, such as it was, she had seemed to go to great lengths to avoid any sort of contact with either him or any other member of Triad. For her to contact him now, and for the second time, no less, she must be in truly a desperate position indeed. Either that, or her overarching plan needed his buy-in, something that he wouldn't put past her, but he had no intention of being someone's pawn, regardless of their end game.

"I'm not sure I can do that," he said after a short pause. "Your cards have made quite a mess and pose a pretty big threat to many people.

"As I'm sure you understand," he explained, "it's my job to make sure that people like that are stopped. I can't just overlook it because you've returned." He chuckled and added, "No matter how nicely you ask."

The tracing program showed its progress as a series of lines with bounce points, places where the call had touched down onto a major hub, highlighted in red. So far, the call had moved through more than twenty bounce points, including three on Lovus itself. He wondered whether that was significant, whether it meant that she was near Lovus. He shook his head and smiled. The woman he had been studying was far too intelligent for that. She just wanted him to *think* she was nearby. He wondered if that was just her natural protocol or if she was showing off.

Either way, he was duly impressed.

"I understand that, of course," she answered breezily. "I would never dream of interfering with Triad and the safety of the people you protect. It's quite a job, and I admire how smoothly you manage all of it."

"Thank you," he said, surprised and a little confused at her praise. It wasn't meant as flattery; despite the flirtatious manner she was speaking in, it had been spoken matter-of-factly. Of course, he reasoned, she has experience being in charge of large groups. Nowhere near as large as the millions of people that comprised the bulk of Triad, of course, but she surely understood the difficulty in keeping any size of an operation functioning smoothly.

"I also agree that the cards responsible for the damage should be dealt with. That's actually why I wanted to speak with you directly. I can't trust the word of any of your men, they don't speak for Triad.

"You, on the other hand, are in a position to make a deal."

"A deal?" he asked, surprised. She couldn't possibly be considering surrender, could she? His troops hadn't gotten anywhere near her or her base on Cardiss, so there was no reason for her to want a plea already. "What kind of deal?"

"I am simply not capable of containing enough of the wanted cards with any reasonable assurance that they wouldn't be able to escape and cause even more trouble. What I would like is to be able to hand them over to your people for safekeeping."

Ryan sat back, stunned at her request. "You'd be willing to hand your people over?" he asked. "Just like that?"

"Of course not," she chuckled. "I wouldn't be handing *my* people over at all." Her voice took a hard edge as she explained. "I dislike the trafficking of Roxxy and other drugs in my name, and I intend to put a stop to it, along with the violence that has been plaguing many of the systems that I once had good working relationships with. These both must stop as quickly as possible.

"The ones who have been causing all of the trouble are no longer my people. They have completely violated everything that I and my Deck stand for and are no longer worthy of my trust or my protection.

"I will protect those who are still loyal to me and deserving of my protection, but those who have and continue to threaten both my reputation and my organization will be dealt with accordingly.

"All I ask is for my people to not be prosecuted when they contact your people to arrange the delivery of the fugitives you are seeking."

Ryan relaxed. He had hoped that this discussion would lead to a better outcome than the ones he had seen before him only an hour before, but he had never hoped that it could end this well. "I think arrangements can be made," he said. "As long as your people behave and aren't posing a larger threat than those I have been tasked to intercept, I think we can work together."

The call ended almost immediately after that, with her assurance that she would contact him when her people were ready to deliver on her promise. He looked down at his tracer, surprised for only a moment when it indicated that it had located the source of the call. Somehow, he had thought her more careful than that.

His surprise changed to outright humor as he recognized where the call had been traced to and he laughed out loud as he picked up the intercom to contact Coffee.

"Don't bother organizing a search for her," he said, predicting his assistant's response to the program's results. He picked up one of the playing cards and looked at it thoughtfully.

"I can guarantee that she is *not* in my office." He sat back in his chair, thoughtful. Given what he knew about the Queen of Diamonds, it was no surprise that she was interested in regaining control of her Deck and minimizing the damage they had been responsible for in her absence. The interest she had expressed in reducing the Roxxy trade, on the other hand, had come as a surprise.

It did, however, remind him of something Coffee had said when the gift basket had first arrived, something about drugs reducing on the planet the rogues had been stranded on. If she and her partner had indeed been responsible for reducing the drug trade on that world, then perhaps it made sense for them to want to reduce it in the greater galaxy as well.

"Are you going home?" Coffee asked as he slipped into Ryan's office. "It had looked like you were about ready to leave when she called."

Ryan shook his head as he switched his computer back on. "I think I want to look into this a little more. You don't need to stay, though. I'll see you tomorrow."

"If you're sure..." Coffee looked hesitant as he agreed. When there was no response from his boss, he exited as quietly as he had entered.

Just because he had asked Coffee to search for information on the planet Diamond and Knave had been stranded on didn't mean that Ryan was incapable of performing the search himself. It took only seconds for him to find the information he was looking for.

The drug traffic on Earth had indeed taken a substantial drop while the pair had been there and had been slowly increasing since their departure. The only rational conclusion was that they had been as responsible as Ryan suspected for the drop. When looking at the numbers outside of the planet, however, he noted that there hadn't been much change either before or during their disappearance, so he wondered if they had seen something on Earth that had changed their minds in regard to the drug trade during their exile.

Regardless of their reasons for doing so, he believed her assertion that they intended to reduce the Roxxy trade. Even if it was only a means to the end of diminishing their opponent's income, that was good enough for him. He would, however, need to keep an eye on what happened after they reclaimed their operation.

CHAPTER

18

TERROS SWEET TERROS

The Knave of Spades and Queen of Diamonds returned to their personal base, located on yet another planet. Terros was in the same system as Ghiel and Majapa, indeed their property on Terros had been one of the deciding factors in the locations of their other two bases.

Their property on Terros was less of a base than it was a summer home. It was a stand of acreage that they had purchased as a getaway many years before, long before their exile and at the beginning of their assembly of the original Deck. Given all that had happened since the purchase of that small area, they were glad that they had kept it a secret from even their closest associates within the Deck. That secrecy guaranteed that none of the usurper's men knew of its existence, exactly what Diamond and Knave needed right then.

The house itself was large: four stories in height and had almost a dozen rooms sprawling out in wings from the central entrance. It had been a vibrant shade of blue thirteen years ago when Diamond had last seen it, but the color had faded over time to be a dusty violet-grey. She eyed the paint critically.

"What are you thinking?" Knave broke into her thoughts.

"Paint's faded," she responded without looking at him."

"It's just paint," he shrugged. "We can get someone out here easily enough to refresh it."

"No," she decided finally. "I think I like this color."

Inside were mementos from many of their early heists. She and Knave had added to the collection throughout the years, so now it contained thousands of priceless artifacts from countless cultures. Each room held at least a half-dozen items that would draw a healthy amount of bidding should they be put up for auction, but the collection was nowhere near the fortune they had once amassed. Each of their memento items either stood atop its own pedestal just over waist-height to Diamond or hung from the wall, perfectly positioned for optimum viewing. Each had its own glasssteel enclosure to keep it from dust and other pollutants and had remained as clean during their exile as they had been before the pair left to steal the Zoscarian crown jewels. Small brass plaques on the front or side of each case identified each item, along with where and when it had been acquired. Now, she realized, should any of her worst-case-scenarios come to pass, she and Knave could find buyers across the galaxy and make enough from the collection they still had to survive in relative comfort for the rest of their lives.

She didn't expect that to happen, however. The cards on Majapa had already uncovered a couple of areas that were primed for picking, both in the Ravenstar system. She had just finished ordering people to infiltrate the area, so hopefully there would be more income soon. So long as those opportunities panned out, she wouldn't have to part with any of her treasured collection.

Knave often teased Diamond that she was allergic to not having money of some variety or another. Although she argued back playfully, they both knew it to be true. That allergy was one of the main reasons she had expanded from their original penny-ante scams that, though they provided food on their table and a roof over their heads, never made quite enough for them to live in relative comfort.

She had spent most of her developing years without two credits to rub together and was determined to never let that happen to her again. So far, the only time that she had come close to breaking that personal oath had been when she and Knave had crashed onto Earth, a planet that had treated her better, and more fairly, than her home world had.

"Those people who were kind enough to bring us a new ship," she thought aloud as she placed a pair of columns opposite each other in the entryway. She didn't have plaques for the new additions to her collection, but those were easy enough to acquire. "I wonder if they've made it off planet yet."

"No idea," Knave responded although it was obvious that his response wasn't necessary. "Do you want to go back to check on them and see if they're still there?"

"Not a chance." Diamond and Knave both knew that if they did decide to return to Earth, and if the original owners of their ship were still there, there was a very real chance that they would steal their ship back, and she wasn't about to let that happen. She walked to one of the cases Knave had carried into the house and withdrew a small, tissue-wrapped package.

She also wondered about deVann and the other men on the task force who had been assigned to capture her and Knave. "I wonder how long it will take for the task force to be disbanded and whether any copycats have popped up." As she unwrapped it, the package revealed a small golden bird, the last item they had stolen from Earth and one of the few trinkets they had brought home with them. Not only did the bird serve as a memento, a souvenir of their involuntary vacation, but it also served as a reminder to keep caution in mind, regardless of how simple and straightforward a task appeared to be on the surface. She arranged the bird on the pedestal, standing back to check the angle and how the light from the high arch of windows that soared above the front door bounced off its body.

That was another peculiarity about the planet they had been stranded on; pretty much anyone who became famous, whether from legal activities or illegal, would develop people who were determined to emulate them. When people tried to copy infamous crimes, particularly murders, they were hunted with the same determination as the original perpetrator would have been. In some cases, the planet's constables arrested the copier instead of the original and found them guilty of all the crimes, regardless of how many the perpetrator had actually been involved with.

She had never understood the term copycat; she wasn't sure what small household feline pets had to do with copying *anything*, but she understood that there was a very real possibility that the men on the force could be chasing many different versions of both herself and Knave at that particular moment.

"Do you really think we can trust Commander Moore?" she mused, more to herself than to anyone else. Happy with the placement of the bird, she settled the glassteel case over it and locked it into place. Only she and Knave had the correct fingerprints to open the cases once sealed, and she intended to keep it that way.

"Bit too late to rethink that, isn't it?"

"I know. But he's law enforcement, after all, and if I was in his place, I wouldn't hesitate to arrest anyone that got too close." From another case, she withdrew a large ornate box. This one held an assortment of jewelry and regalia from the heist that had started the chase resulting in their time on Earth. It seemed only fitting that it should be displayed near the bird, a testament to the beginning and end of that particular adventure.

"True. Doesn't make sense that he would stay in a position like Commander for very long if he just let his targets escape all the time." Without needing to be asked, he handed her a velvet-covered display stand. More than just the excitement of the heists, which she clearly enjoyed, being able to sit back and enjoy the fruits of her labor was what really made her happy, particularly when that labor was for additions to her personal collection rather than just for resale value.

"Exactly." She flopped into an overstuffed armchair to arrange the jewels decoratively on the velvet stand. Originally the theft had been meant for resale, but with everything that had resulted from the heist, she had long since decided that if she ever left Earth, she would keep the treasure for herself. "But he is pretty well known for his integrity. Do you think that extends to us, too?" Despite his reputation, there were reasonable odds that his agreement to her proposal was more than just a bluff, but the bird reminded her clearly to not take everything at face value.

She needed him.

Now all she needed was a way to hand the members of the King's Deck over to Triad without revealing too much of her own hand.

SIGNUS IV

The Deck had been in control of the Signus system for over seven years, mostly due to the presence of a squad of Aces on almost every station scattered throughout the system. On Station Twelve, the space station orbiting the innermost ring of Signus IV, there were more cards than usual but there were more people all together on that station than on any other station in the system.

The station looked very much like a barbell, with a narrow central corridor connecting two large, bulbous spheres. The docking rings were located in the central column and elevators transported crew and visitors from one end of the station to the other. Only a handful of people lived on the station, most were stationed there for a short time.

One of the reasons this station was so heavily guarded, besides its abundance of traffic, was because of the small manufacturing center located on one of its lowermost decks. This laboratory was not known to any save a handful of people assigned to work in it and the guards who ensured their production levels were met. Although this laboratory was not the largest of its kind, it was the most productive one in the Signus system. Once each week, the Roxxy produced in the laboratory was packaged up and sent out for distribution.

Five laborers, dressed in little more than aprons to protect themselves from the harsh chemicals they worked with, moved silently from one station to another, measuring carefully and checking temperatures in the small vats. Fumes from the cooking chemicals vented through a duct overhead out into the void of space. At the door, two men stood guard, each wearing a black uniform with a pair of small club-shaped crystals in their lapels.

A medium-sized transport freighter named *Leviathan*, loaded with goods destined for the nearby Oberron system, was attached to one of the docking rings and the crew and passengers from the ship were gathered on one of the disused lower levels of the station. Normally, in a crowd that size, there would be dozens of discussions and in the acoustics of an open-steel room the buzz of even muted conversations could grow to be almost deafening.

There was silence.

Two of the freighter's crew members, people who were less enthusiastic about the Deck's recruitment policy, lay dead in the middle of the floor. Blood slowly puddled beneath their motionless bodies. The rest of the *Leviathan's* crew and passengers cowered against the far wall as a tall, black-haired man with a scar running horizontally from his left cheekbone into his hair, bisecting his ear, walked calmly in front of the terrified people. Small, club-shaped crystals were set into the lapels of his black uniform and his footsteps echoed loudly from the metallic walls and floor.

"Your options are simple," the Ace explained, "and lay here before you." He stepped over one of the bodies, as if to accentuate his point. "Join us, do as you are instructed, and survive."

He stopped and turned to face his audience, slowly looking down the length of people and making eye contact with as many of his terrified hostages as he could see. "Of course, you can always choose to decline our generous offer," he said with a slight chuckle.

He was not the only Ace in the room. Two more men guarded the room, one with crystal hearts on his shirt and the other with spades. Three more were positioned strategically throughout the room. More Aces guarded the corridor beyond the narrow airlock, so that even if some of the crew and passengers managed to escape past the Aces in the room, they wouldn't make it out of the corridor.

When the door that led to the hallway opened, the Aces and their hostages took no notice. A handful of small silver and blue canisters, each no more than a few tenths of a unit in diameter, flew into the room through the open door. At the same time, one of the air vents overhead opened and more canisters fell through the hatch to the floor more than three units below. The airlock door slammed shut and the sound of the heavy bolt sliding into place echoed through the room.

One canister exploded on impact with an ear-splitting scream and bright, rapidly flashing yellow and white lights. The lights, in turn, became even more disorienting as thick, heavy, terrible-scented smoke, released from more of the canisters, filled the room. Within seconds, vision had been reduced to barely a half unit and every person in the room was gagging on the foul stench, disoriented and screaming in terror.

A third variety of canister, unnoticed in the commotion, slowly began to release its contents. Undetectable beneath the choked room, the odorless gas filtered through the air. Far more potent than even the heady smoke, the gas began to fill the room. Slowly, one by one, the crew members, passengers, and Aces began to slump to the ground, unconscious.

The airlock door opened and a figure, his immense size barely distinguishable in the thick smog, strode into the room. A specially-designed breathing mask, shaped and crafted to cover his nose, mouth, and all three eyes, obscured his face from view and allowed him to breathe the noxious fumes without falling victim to them.

He was dressed in black, similar to the clothing the Aces wore but without any insignia marking rank or status. A closer inspection would reveal that his pants and shirtsleeves were too short for someone of his stature but there was nobody left conscious to discover that the clothes were not tailored for him. A black backpack was slung over one broad shoulder.

A second figure, also dressed in black, dropped gracefully to the floor from the overhead vent, narrowly avoiding landing on one of the deceased men who had been killed by the Aces. A similar mask covered the Emovete's wide green eyes, and they nodded to each other without speaking. Unlike her companion, she wore a single diamond gemstone in her lapel.

In the hall, visible beneath the escaping smoke, Aces slumped against the walls, unconscious and bound with sturdy restraints, lined up on both sides of the hall in much the same fashion as the innocent people inside the room had been. Smears of blood on the walls and the floor, as well as the bruising and painfully twisted limbs on the unconscious men and women, indicated that the hallway guards had not submitted to the attackers' ploy as quickly and easily as the men inside the room had done.

The masked people moved to the Aces first, removing all of their credit sticks, weapons, and other useful tools before binding them with secure ties. All of the contraband equipment went into the Tet's backpack, to be sorted later.

Once all of the Aces were secure, the innocent travelers were dragged and carried, some more easily than others, into the corridor and the remaining Aces were brought, much less gently, into the room. Still more Aces were brought to join their brethren from a laboratory just down the hall. Once everyone was inside, the small woman engaged the airlock, ensuring that the Aces would remain in place and unconscious for some time yet.

The Emovete pressed a button on the side of her mask, which activated her comm unit. "We have people for you," she explained, her voice sounding hollow in the confined space. "They will be waiting on the lowermost level of Station Twelve, orbiting Signus IV.

"You might want to get your people out here before they start waking up."

CHAPTER

20

THE COLLECTION AGENCY

"Captain!" a man dressed in the blue uniform of the Triad recovery unit signaled to his unit leader. "You need to see this."

Stump Numperel was dressed in the same midnight blue uniform as his men, with the addition of a small gold star on his lapel, signifying his rank. He nodded to one of his men to continue debriefing the crew and passengers of the *Leviathan,* a cargo ship that had briefly stopped at the station to resupply and refuel before continuing to the Oberron system. He felt for the people, as it appeared from their statements that they had only narrowly avoided becoming slaves to the marauders who had beset their ship as soon as they had docked on the station. Stump couldn't imagine the fear that they had all felt during their ordeal, but he did find it curious that none of them could explain how they had managed to escape. One moment they had all been huddled in a meeting room where their fates were explained to them and the next, they were back out on their ship with no idea how they had gotten from one point to the next.

He jogged down the narrow corridors, each footfall echoing loudly from the metal walls, wondering for the millionth time why they had to make the halls on every space station so narrow. His shoulders were almost a unit and two tenths across but, because he was only a unit and a half in height, he appeared even wider than he actually was. Under normal circumstances, his girth wasn't a problem but he had to turn sideways to let others pass three times in the forty yards it took him to reach the soldier who had called for his attention.

"What is it" Stump demanded as he walked towards the airlock at the end of the corridor. The young soldier didn't answer, he simply pointed into the room beyond the doorway.

Stump grunted and pushed his way past the young man, making a mental note to have a word with him later about answers being somatic rather than pantomime. While his intention this time was clear, Stump didn't want to risk having any confusion should it happen again elsewhere.

His irritation with the soldier stopped as he stepped into the room, however, and he gave a low whistle of appreciation. "Impressive," he said calmly. "Very impressive."

Almost twenty men and women, all dressed in the scattered outfits that passed for uniforms among the illicit group known as the Deck, were waiting for his arrival. Not that they had much choice in the matter, Stump chuckled to himself. Even if any of them had wanted to escape, which some obviously did, they were well and truly stuck.

They were all bound in a circle; each of them with their hands restrained behind their backs, tied to themselves, each person on either side of them, and to a central ring. "Someone was serious about keeping them from escaping," he said as he walked around the circle.

The captives' feet were spread out in front of them, each foot tied to the foot of the person next to them on either side, so that they formed a multi-faceted star pattern in the center of the floor. Some were obviously uncomfortable in this arrangement, as many had legs of differing lengths, some of whose feet didn't quite reach the next person in line and such were attached to their neighbor's knees. They squirmed in discomfort, movements that Stump ignored. His attention had been drawn elsewhere in the room.

Two bodies lay on the ground just beyond the captured cards, stuck fast to the metal floor by the dried blood that once kept them alive. Overhead, a pair of playing cards dangled from the exit of a ventilation shaft, fluttering in the slight breeze.

"Whatever else they may be," Stump smiled to himself as he watched the cards dance in midair, "they got style."

He turned back to the door, calling his superior officer as he went. "I guess they weren't kidding about handing these people over, boss," he explained. "We've got over a dozen of them here waiting for us, and a pair of calling cards to boot."

CHAPTER

21

SLOW GROWTH

The Queen of Diamonds was growing frustrated. For the last six months, she had been chipping away at the King's Deck and expanding her own base of power. Over a hundred cards had been turned over to Triad and the base on Majapa continued to grow. The base on Ghiel, on the other hand, remained with only a few more members than the handful of people they had started with. Misdirecting information had been passed through them to keep the cards loyal to the King of Clubs running in circles, chasing at shadows.

Old contacts were back in the fold and a handful of new contacts had been made as well. As much as Diamond didn't like dealing with Protus any more often than absolutely necessary, he had become a staple on Majapa and his presence had proven invaluable for assessing new contacts and recruits. Given his particular position, he hadn't brought her any new contacts, but he had been willing to verify all of the contacts she and her cards had made in order to ensure that none of them were playing both sides of the game. Only a few of them had shown themselves to be dubious.

However, for all that had been done so far, Diamond didn't feel that she had done very much at all to take her empire back from the stranglehold the King of Clubs held over it. He had continued to expand, continued to recruit, and continued to be as large a threat as ever. More so, despite all of her efforts to curtail the Roxxy distribution, the drugs continued to be as much of a problem as ever. What she had initially expected to be a difficult takeover of her Deck had proven to be much more than she had planned for.

Worse, she realized, was that they couldn't even be certain that the King of Clubs was at the original home base of the Deck on Cardiss. Surely, knowing how easily he could move from one location to another and keep his position secure, he had relocated to a more remote and secretive location. She had spent most of the last two months searching for any sign of where he might be, but there was nothing. She would continue to search, but the truth was becoming clearly, painfully obvious.

She had no idea where he was and, unless her situation drastically improved, she had no way of finding him.

Initially, she and Knave had tried to question some of the cards that they had captured but either the interrogated cards had no information to give, or they were far more afraid of the King than they were of Knave and Diamond.

She had to admit that the cards' position was a sensible one, even if she didn't like it. No matter what they did to the captured cards, everyone knew that they wouldn't be killed... a promise that wasn't held by the King and his men, should they discover the cards had folded. In almost every interrogation she had observed, the cards had pleaded to their interrogators for mercy, explaining that should the king discover their betrayal, not only their own lives were at stake, but the lives of their family, friends, and teammates as well.

So now she found herself in the unenviable position of trying to think of new ways to move on the King's cards, but she found herself lacking. Not lacking, precisely, for she had plenty of good ideas left. Instead, she found herself without any means of inflicting enough damage to the King of Clubs and his Deck to hurt them with the rather limited means she had at her disposal.

"I have an idea."

She looked up as the voice penetrated her thoughts, surprised that Knave had managed to sneak up on her like that. For as large of a man as he was, he could move with remarkable silence when he desired. It had been years since he had been able to do so, and it had turned into more of a game than anything else.

Now, seeing how bothered she was, and how particularly unfocused to have let him come so close without realizing it, Knave's expression darkened into one of worry. He held out the cup of tea that he had brought for her and sat onto a seat to her left.

She took a sip of the warm brew, realizing that he had either been standing behind her for longer than she had thought or that he had waited for the drink to cool before bringing it to her. When he had first offered her the cup, she had been concerned that it may have been one of his dark black teas, but she was relieved to discover it was a soothing lemon, lavender, and chamomile blend. Even better, it was the perfect drinking temperature.

"What's your idea?" she asked as she took another sip of the drink.

"Actually," he said, his voice oddly hesitant, "it's less of an idea than it is a confession."

She arched an eyebrow and looked at him expectantly.

"I already contacted the Vergling government," he explained, his expression sheepish. "I offered them the sale of the weapons and a couple of warships that have been taken from the King of Clubs."

She looked at her friend, appalled. "You did what?" she asked, her voice barely above a whisper and quivering with horror. "How could you do that? We don't deal in death; you know that!"

"I know," he said, his eyes downcast, "and I knew you wouldn't like that I was doing it. That's why I didn't ask you first."

She was speechless. For years, he had stood by her side, the brother she never had, the only family she had ever known, which meant that this betrayal was more than painful. It was a sharp, deep wound into a heart that was already covered with so much scar tissue that it was barely recognizable. In her life, betrayal was inevitable from almost every corner, but the last person she would have expected it from was Knave.

"They accepted," he continued without looking up at her, "which gave us a better financial standing. You were asking the other day why there were so many credits in the accounts, so I knew I had to come tell you before you finished searching the records and found out for yourself."

At his admission, Diamond fought to get herself back under control, to hide the furious *tress* that had burned across her body. She remembered the conversation he was referring to and realized with a start exactly how much more money he had brought in as a result of his actions.

And he was right, she admitted. Not about selling the weapons, which she could never condone. No, he was right to tell her himself. It would have been far worse had her search led her to his actions.

How much more betrayed would she have felt then? She reasoned with herself.

It didn't matter, she realized. Whether she had agreed to it or not, what he had done didn't matter. It wasn't something that could be changed. It had already happened.

Besides, there were worse things he could have done. While he admitted to selling the Verglings weapons, he hadn't sold them any of the ammunition, rendering the weapon sales almost irrelevant given the exorbitant cost of ammunition lately. He hadn't armed their people, an idea that she had turned down flat when the Ten of Clubs had suggested it on their last trip to Majapa. And there were far worse people that Knave could have sold the warships and weapons to as well.

At least the Verglings were fighting against the Deck, or at least the jackals who were still using their name, so the weapons and ships that Diamond and Knave's Deck had taken would be used against those who used them in the first place. There was a sense of ironic justice in it, she thought as her mind and body calmed. They had no use for them, so all they had been doing was using up valuable storage space and personnel to guard them.

"Also," he continued as her *tress* continued to fade from view, "I contacted Triad to request their assistance in the Oberron system."

Knave's initiative to contact Triad, despite his usual insistence that she be the person contacting them, was not much of a surprise. It was unreasonable for anyone to expect all communication to come from Diamond directly and the entire galaxy, at least those who had reason to know of the pair's existence, knew that he operated under her authority. Even if that meant using that authority to sell warships. However, his request struck her as an unlikely one at best.

"You think they'll get involved?" She looked up at him, not bothering to hide the pain in her eyes. "Oberron has never even entertained the idea of joining the Interplanetary Government. Triad's not going to go out and help someone that isn't part of the IG. They aren't even allies." Although Triad had been challenged to take down the Deck, she wasn't certain of their ability to act outside of IG territory.

"But they are allies of a sort, in an indirect way. Triad has millions of ships that run on Myrite. Since their source of fuel is endangered by the fake King's presence in Oberron, Triad will act to preserve its own supply line, if for no other reason."

She looked up at him doubtfully. "I'm not as positive about that as you are," she said. "There are tons of other sources of Myrite, so this won't affect Triad as much as you think it will." She thought for a moment, considering her options. "But maybe we can tip their hand, even if they don't play."

She activated the communication console and connected to the Ghiel base. "Get in touch with all of your contacts," she explained as soon as her call was answered, "and allies. Tell them to move as far away from the Oberron system as they can."

"What's going on?" a voice on the other end asked. Diamond didn't recognize who the voice belonged to, but it didn't matter. As long as the word got out.

"Triad's on their way," she embellished. "Get as many of our people out of the way as we can." She cut the comm link immediately, leaving no room for questions.

"What if Triad doesn't show up?" Knave asked, echoing her doubts.

"This can go one of four ways," she replied. "First, Triad agrees to assist in Oberron and the King of Clubs will focus his resources in that area to try and block them. When Triad shows, up, those resources will be annihilated." She didn't like the idea that she was discussing the deaths of countless people, but the probability couldn't be ignored.

"Second, the cards pull back and concede the lines, in which case we can work to create an alliance with the Verglings." That was her favorite of the available options, but she thought the chances of it happening were slim at best. Still, one couldn't help but hold out hope.

"Third," she ticked them off on her fingers as she explained, "Triad doesn't show up after they consolidate their lines, and the Verglings use the weapons you sold them to hold them off." Since they had sold those weapons and warships to the Verglings, she already felt responsible for any damage that would result and hoped that this particular situation wouldn't come to pass.

"And finally, the so-called-King moves his people back in anticipation of Triad showing up, so when they get there, there's no resistance." She looked up at her friend as she was finished. "All four of these options put us on stronger standing than we are right now."

"What if they withdraw?" he asked. "Won't that just give them more troops to use against us?"

She nodded solemnly. "Yes, it would." She took another drink of the tea he had brought for her. A peace offering, she realized, that's what it was. He had known how badly she would react to what he had come in to tell her and had brought the tea specifically because of it.

He knew her too well, she realized. But then, don't most families know each other that well? Not that she had much to reference the idea against, of course. Knave had been her only family for about as long as she could remember.

"It's a gamble," she admitted. "I think we'll just have to hope that they'll be too greedy to pull back." Much as she didn't want to see any of the king's cards killed by either Triad or Vergling troops, it was the easiest way to soften their impact in the Oberron system. The scant handful of people she had available would not be enough to make much of a dent in that battle line should their tactics fail.

After she finished both her conversation with Knave and her cup of tea, she called the Ten of Spades on Majapa. "Send a team to take the crystal mines," she ordered once he was on the phone, "and another to the palladium mines. I think it's time to start moving on both locations." Both places had been targets identified in the latest round of soft spots located by the Majapan cards. Steram, a nondescript planet in the Ravenstar system, possessed a thick atmosphere perfect for growing the ultra-clear crystals used in the manufacture of spaceships. As a result, it had a small but productive crystal mine that was fully operational. The best part was that because the mining operation was so new, it had only the barest of minimal security in place so overtaking the small area wouldn't be too difficult with just a small team of cards.

The palladium mines she knew would be a much bigger challenge. They were located on Ralund, the lesser moon of Tegintys, which was also in the Ravenstar system. Unlike the new, barely-operational crystal mines, the palladium mines were well underway and had plenty of guards stationed everywhere. They also had almost no discernable atmosphere, conditions that were exceptionally difficult to work with. Be that as it may, she had faith that her teams would prove successful in both operations. Both of those hazards understood, the palladium mines were still a far better target, since the valuable material was used in almost every electronic device used across the galaxy. Even an ounce of the precious metal could be sold at a premium, and the mine promised more than just an ounce.

Along with the recommendation to take both areas, the Ten of Spades had sent a report on how both could be done, simultaneously if needed. He had already begun placing cards into valuable positions in both locations and now the security force surrounding the mines of Ralund were comprised of almost sixty percent cards sent by the Ten. The idea of carrying out both of the operations at the same time appealed to Diamond, even though she understood it to be a challenge to the people who were sent to pull it off.

With the King of Clubs and his cards focused on Oberron, Diamond's Deck should be able to overtake both areas, creating a foothold in the Ravenstar system at the same time. When both the crystal and palladium mines were under her control, she and Knave would soon have access to enough funds to pay for the rest of her plans. She walked thoughtfully to the kitchen and fixed herself another cup of tea. This was about to get very exciting, indeed.

KILL ORDERS

The King of Clubs was livid. Too many of his troops had been taken out by the cards who had moved to the so-called Queen's Deck, and nobody even knew where the imposters who dared to call themselves the Queen of Diamonds and Knave of Spades even *were.*

He had just been handed a report on troop movement in the Ravenstar system and what he read within that report was almost beyond belief. "How?" He howled in frustration as he flung the papers against a far wall. The loose papers struck the wall with a soft thump before fluttering to the ground. "How do they keep moving like that?" He stood and began to stalk back and forth across the room, looking more like a vicious, tormented predator than the undisputed leader of the most successful piracy operation ever known.

"What happened now?" his Ace asked. The Ace of Diamonds had, by his own suggestion, replaced himself as a leader of the assault squadron fighting in the Oberron system and had instead focused on creating a protection detail around the King.

"They're in Ravenstar," the King snarled, his voice almost incomprehensible in his rage. "They took over a couple of key portions of the Ravenstar system, positions that we needed to maintain our hold on the rest of the system." The loss of the crystal mine in particular troubled him as he had spent the better part of a year maneuvering his cards to sweep in and take control as soon as it was operational, a plan that had been thwarted even before it began. It was the fourth time plans such as that had been yanked out from beneath his feet and he still had no clue how they were doing it.

"Do you know what this means?" he demanded as he rushed forward, only to stop a fraction of a unit away from the unconcerned Ace.

"It means you are angry, your highness," the Ace answered smoothly. "But are you certain that it was Diamond and Knave who took these areas from you?"

"Who else could it be?" he stalked across the room again, wishing he had something to smash. The walls of his room were only thin plaster over solid steel, so punching a wall wouldn't do him any good. All of the breakables that had once been housed in his personal living quarters had either been taken away or destroyed in one of his fits already, so the only things left in the room were his teak table and his overstuffed chair. The table had been specially made for him, inlaid with gold, bright accents to offset the dark wood. The chair was equally dark, made of buttery-soft worked leather that conformed to his body every time he sat upon it.

He needed the table.

He liked the chair.

He needed new decorations, he decided. Lots of heavy vases to throw and sculptures to knock asunder. Maybe even a tapestry or two that he could rip to shreds. The only thing he had left available to him was a painting which had become a dartboard some months before. A small handful of garnet-colored darts were still embedded in the artwork, the frame, and mostly in the wall around it. Darts had never been his weapon of choice and his terrible aim only served as a reminder of why he belonged as the leader of the Deck instead of just the low-level soldier he had been years before.

The best thing that had ever happened to him, he realized, was for the Queen of Diamonds to disappear. Even better, she had taken her pet Spade with her, wherever she had gone. That was why these rumors of their return were so unsettling to him. While at first he had been adamant that they were all lies, the more he witnessed their undermining of his operation, the more inclined he was to believe that perhaps there was more than just rumor and impersonation involved. Who else would be both brazen and skillful enough to have pulled off so many stunts as they had?

"Of course, there's no proof," he admitted finally as he sunk into his chair. Despite the lack of proof, he was certain that the Queen of Diamonds and Knave of Spades were responsible. They were just too tricky, that was his problem. He had sent Aces out across the galaxy in an attempt to find out where they were, but there had been no sign of either of them.

Or almost no sign, he corrected himself. The only confirmed sightings of them he had received stemmed from their occasional visits to Ghiel, but even those had been limited in number. From what his spies on Ghiel had reported, the people trying to take his empire away from him matched every description of the infamous duo available, right down to what few tactics his people had uncovered.

Not that they had uncovered much, of course. As usual, Diamond and Knave were working from behind a smokescreen, so he had no idea what they were up to. Even when they had still been in charge of everything from Cardiss out, very few people had truly understood everything they were up to at any given time.

In many cases, it had taken years for people to discover the true effects of the pair's machinations.

"As if that wasn't bad enough," he complained as he snatched up a paper that had landed close to his seat, "my people in Ghiel intercepted a message last week."

"What kind of message?" the Ace asked politely.

"Triad's on its way to the Oberron system," he growled from between clenched teeth. "They're on their way to help those filthy, stinking Verglings." If there was one race in the entire galaxy he hated, it was the Verglings. The insectoids raised a deep, visceral reaction in him whenever he so much as thought about them. He just couldn't understand how a group so massive, so populous, could possibly be as intelligent and effective when there was only one creature in their entire community that had a functioning mind. All of the Verglings he had ever encountered had simply been drones, a sort of extension or puppet of the only self-aware and conscious Vergling in the bunch.

"What do you intend to do?"

The King barked in laughter. "What *can* I do?" he asked. "All I can do is send in reinforcements, so of course I'm going to send reinforcements. Seven *squads* of reinforcements. I can't afford to lose this operation now." It was probably more than he needed to send, likely more than he should have sent, but they were necessary. If they lost the Myrite mining operation in the Oberron system, none of it would matter anymore. Everything he had planned rested on his ability to gain and maintain control of the Myrite supply. Without that, he may as well just disband the whole operation because it would become effectively useless.

Well, he considered his options, *maybe not completely useless.* While his Roxxy supply and distribution had also taken a substantial hit, there was far more to that operation than what had been taken. Additionally, his scientists had created a new formula, with more powerful effects, that was about to be released.

The fact that the new formula, which they had begun calling ZB-2 for unfathomable reasons, was many times more addictive than Roxxy was an added bonus. The ZB-2 was originally supposed to have been distributed from the Signus system, but Diamond and her team had made that plan impossible.

Thankfully he had a fallback plan for distribution, one they had not yet managed to thwart.

"Understandable, your highness," the Ace responded automatically. "If I could make a suggestion."

The King of Clubs sighed. Here it came. He was fairly certain that this particular Ace delighted in pointing out things that the King had overlooked. Almost every time they spoke, the Ace of Diamonds had a suggestion, which was almost always thinly veiled criticism.

It certainly didn't help that he was usually right. In fact, that was one of the few reasons that the King kept the irritating Ace around.

That, and the fact that he was afraid of him. Not much, and not all the time, but there was always the tiny shiver of fear at the back of his neck when he thought about exactly how many deaths this man was responsible for, most of whom he had killed with his own bare hands. The King of Clubs was a brawler, there was no doubt about that, but he had been trained for intrigue more than assassination so he wasn't sure how a fight between himself and this Ace, or any Ace for that matter, would end.

And he wasn't eager to find out, either.

"You remember, of course," the Ace continued without waiting to see if the King was interested in hearing his suggestion, "that we have an Ace already in position with the rebels on Ghiel."

The King blinked in surprise. He had forgotten, actually. Slowly, he blinked in thought, grudgingly recognizing the logic in the Ace's thinly-veiled recommendation. "Yes, I suppose it would be easy enough to issue a kill order."

"Indeed, your highness." The Ace's voice was as smooth as silk and as deadly as a razor blade. "Shall I send the word?"

The King nodded silently. He didn't hate the Queen of Diamonds, much as she aggravated him by thwarting almost every move he made. He had merely stepped into power at her disappearance and didn't want to hand what he believed was his organization by rights back over to her because she had reappeared.

He had served loyally under her for years while she had still been in power, although he had never achieved a rank higher than six, far below his own ability level, as he had proven since then. He rose in the years after her disappearance to the rank of nine, and from that position he advanced himself to king when he took control of the Deck.

The Ace was right, as usual. He couldn't allow her to live if he wanted to maintain and expand his own operation. He was losing people left and right, they were flocking to her in droves, and there was nothing he could do to stop it.

Well, almost nothing.

"Send the order," he said. His voice was low and solemn. "The next time she steps foot on Ghiel, kill her.

"Just be sure to take Knave down first," he added. "He's the more dangerous, physically, of the two."

"Oh, and while you're sending orders," he called as the Ace headed for the door, "I think we need to step up the recruitment as well. We're going to need more people."

CHAPTER

23

GROWING PAINS

"I think it's time to expand," Diamond explained to Knave over breakfast.

"Already?" he asked as he took a bite of his food.

She nodded. "Majapa's not going to be able to hold many more cards, so whether we expand the Majapan base or find a new one altogether, we need to do something."

He nodded and chewed thoughtfully. "A new one would probably bring less attention." After another bite, he asked, "Were you thinking about any place in particular?"

She shook her head, curls bouncing off her cheeks as she moved. "There are a lot of places we could go," she said, "but none of them seem very appealing."

"How about Ziloc?" he suggested after another bite. The omelet was no longer as appealing as it had seemed when he first woke, but since he didn't like to waste food, it would be consumed before he left the table. He just wished Diamond would stop using the fire peppers in so many of the foods she had him eat. "It's a pretty small system but its nearer to Cardiss than any of the other bases. That would grant us a better launching point for hitting closer to the King of Clubs' main operating areas when you decide we're ready to do that." He tried to pick out at least a few of the peppers, but they all seemed to be encapsulated in cheese and other ingredients, making their removal all but impossible.

Diamond took a bite of her own omelet, savoring the sweet mushrooms and spicy peppers as she pondered his idea. It sounded logical enough and Ziloc, one of the smaller systems that bordered Xerxes, was already on her short list of areas into which she wanted to expand. "Even better," she said, "It's close enough to the Oberron system that we can monitor the activity there and see how the battle goes."

The more she thought about it, the better it sounded. Finally, she nodded and Knave finished his food, picked up his half-finished cup of tea, and went out to make the call. Once she was gone, she giggled softly to herself, noticing the small pile of fire peppers he had left on the side of his plate. For a Tet, he sure couldn't handle his spicy foods at all. That simply meant that there was more spice for her to enjoy.

Thinking about the Oberron system reminded her about the military action that they had helped support. She still wasn't happy about their decision to team up with Triad, but she had to admit that it was for a good cause. Given how many cards she had turned over for incarceration, she knew that they didn't have enough room on all of their bases combined to hold that many people.

Another thing that she grudgingly accepted involved one of their more lucrative income streams. She was fairly certain that Knave had continued to broker deals with the Verglings for the sale and disposition of more weapons, as there had been three separate occasions where the credits in their accounts had increased noticeably but, thankfully, Knave had neglected to mention the source to her.

She supposed she was just looking the other way, in a rather obvious manner of speaking. She wasn't pleased with the way things had begun working, but she couldn't deny that the credits were badly needed and there was no real use for the weapons they confiscated.

She further supposed that they could have tried to sell them to Triad, if they were going to sell them at all, but the idea of selling someone weapons that could end up being used against her and her people just seemed like a bad idea. At least the Verglings understood to not attack her people during their wars.

"Do you think it's time to weed out the spies on Ghiel?" she asked Knave when he returned. "I'm starting to think that they aren't quite as valuable as we had originally expected them to be." The spies that Protus had identified had remained in their positions on the Ghiel base and Diamond had sent a fairly constant stream of mostly useless information their way to keep the King of Clubs from interfering with more of her operations. With the amount of growth they had experienced, as well as their partnerships with the Verglings and Triad, she was no longer certain that they were worth the risk of keeping them in place. She had wanted to remove them and hand them over to Triad the last few times they had been on the base, but the timing hadn't felt quite right yet. Now, however, it felt like she was ready."

"I think that's reasonable." He had wanted to remove the Ghiel traitors long ago and had already compiled a list of the people who had failed Protus's examination. With Diamond's apparent readiness to cull the herd, it would only take one order to the Ten of Spades to remove all of the offenders from their positions and have them sent to lockup until they could be transported to hand over to Triad. Knave hadn't been particularly fond of the idea of keeping them on the base for as long as they had been there and was pleased that she had finally come to her senses. Keeping that many people loyal to the King of Clubs nearby caused him to constantly worry about her safety.

Just shy of a week after their expansion conversation, Diamond and Knave travelled to Majapa to arrange the movement of about a third of the standing cards to their new base. Knave had located a perfect place on Mota, a small planetoid in the Ziloc system, and after a brief inspection she had authorized the purchase. While Knave gathered those who had been selected to change bases and promoted a new Ten and set of Nines, Diamond met with Ten of Spades to inquire about the progress that had been made so far on the assignments he had been given.

"Takeovers on the palladium and crystal mines went well," he reported proudly.

"Injuries?"

"None," he answered even more proudly than before, and Diamond's opinion of the man she had placed in charge increased dramatically. To have pulled off a pair of operations like those, even considering the amount of preparations he had done before starting, was impressive in and of itself. To have done so without injuries was even more so.

"How long before exports can begin?" she inquired.

"Already started." His grin, impossibly, had stretched even wider, so that it seemed as though his face would soon be split in half. "At least," he corrected himself, "palladium is already being exported. There were a few hitches reported from the crystal mines, so the mining isn't fully operational there yet, but my people are taking care of them."

Diamond was pleased with his news for multiple reasons. Perhaps some of those mysterious deposits weren't all from Knave selling weapons after all. "What's going on with the crystal mines?"

"Apparently the King of Clubs wanted a piece of the action, too. A small team of soldiers from his Deck showed up shortly after we took control."

Diamond was surprised. Not that the King had wanted another piece of her pie, but that the Ten's people had been able to rebuff their advance without injury.

"Some of the locals knew who they were," the Ten explained. "They decided that working with us was a much better option, so they stood with us against them. There were a couple of injuries to them," he confessed, "but nothing that couldn't be handled with minor medical attention."

Once their business on Majapa was concluded, Diamond and Knave traveled to Ghiel. Against Knave's objections, Diamond had decided to check on how she felt about the spies on the lunar base before making her final decision on whether or not it was time to reveal them. There, they called a meeting of their ranking officers. Just in case, he had his list of traitors in his pocket, ready to hand over to the Ten if she decided it was time after all.

"We're planning to expand soon," Diamond explained. "For now, we're looking at possible locations in the Yareth system. We need you to start looking at the areas there and make at least two recommendations."

Even as the five officers in the room began to discuss which planets, moons, and space stations located in Yareth would make a good location for a new base, the door burst open and gunfire erupted through the room. A short, stocky man dressed in all black with crystal hearts glinting at his lapel followed the path of the bullets into the room and aimed more directly at Knave and Diamond, who were both sitting at the head of the meeting table.

For a fraction of a second, time stopped for Diamond and everything fell silent.

She had waited too long.

Screams replaced chatter as everyone dove for the floor in a mass of confusion and terror. The Dolrathi, one of the original members of Diamond's resistance, shrieked in pain as two rounds entered their lower body mass. Bullets ricocheted off the walls of the room, most reflecting back into the room to embed themselves aimlessly in the meeting table, still-spinning chairs, and floor, some hitting the group who had been so calm and satisfied only moments before. Trying to stay focused, Diamond marveled that one of the assailants had aimed so badly as to hit the smallest target in the room, one that was already so close to the ground. She held no doubts that the lethal projectiles were intended for herself and Knave.

Someone grabbed her arm and Diamond looked up to her left, meeting not the steady brown trio of eyes she had expected but instead the green-flecked gaze of the Nine of Clubs. "We have to get you out of here," the Club hissed through her teeth. "Follow me."

She gave no room for argument as she half led, half dragged Diamond towards a small, unassuming door at the back of the room. Raising herself only high enough to grasp the knob, the Club shoved the door open and Diamond through it.

The narrow corridor, one of the maintenance channels that spider-webbed this and all planetary bases, was filled with people. Four armed men quickly surrounded Diamond and a quick look behind her confirmed her suspicions as she watched the Nine of Clubs close and lock the door.

There would be no help from inside the meeting room – at least, none that would arrive on time.

"You've caused more than enough of a disruption already" one of her assailants said in a rough, guttural voice. "We can't allow you to expand your operation, or to continue damaging the King's operation.

"The way we all figure it, you've been dead for thirteen years now, so forcing you to live up to that particular reputation should be no problem." A pair of crystalline clubs shone on his shirt, catching Diamond's eye.

He slowly raised his weapon, a high-caliber Gasjet pistol and aimed for the head of the Queen of Diamonds.

TICO'S NIGHTMARE

Every day had been the same. The smell of oil, the hard crunch of gravel, the permeating mist of old, stale cigars. The scene was the same, no matter where Tico was brought. Everywhere was exactly the same.

Tico wasn't her real name; she had no idea what her real name had been. It didn't matter. Her owner called her Tico, and she had quickly learned to respond.

She had quickly learned to do a lot.

Tico wound the thin, stretchy bands of tape around her hands, the only concession her owner would allow her when she was scheduled for a match. She wasn't allowed shoes, as far as she could remember she had never worn a pair, so her feet were thick, hardened slabs of callous and scars. Her fighting trunks were new, or at least newer than anything else she owned. The deep, forest green shorts with a bright yellow stripe down each thigh were exactly the same every time she got a new pair and she had long since stopped bothering to notice whether the shorts were new or not.

Her once bright green eyes were dull and listless, belying the amount of attention she was truly paying to everything that was happening around her. Even though the scene was always the same, she kept a close watch for any telltale signs of difference, of mood, of anything pointing towards change. A swift, sharp pinch on her left bicep told her that the referee had taken his sample to test for illegal substances, performance enhancers, which would give her an edge.

She never needed them.

She hadn't started out as the person to beat. Just like everyone else, she had started out as a nobody, the new whelp for even the lowest fighter in the circuit to rise just a little bit in the standings.

She hadn't stayed there for long.

To everyone's surprise – everyone except her owner, of course – she had risen through the ranks like a bottle rocket, cutting down everyone who got in her way. Her first three fights had been pathetic, pitted against boys twice her size that could barely even hold a decent guard position, let alone swing a punch.

Soon she had been moved to larger, more expensive arenas. The entrance fees that her owner had to fork over had increased with every bout she fought, but so had the prize money when she won.

Losing had never been an option.

That day, Tico was scheduled to fight Remus, one of the only fighters she had never gone against. He was five years older than her eight and stood over a half unit taller than she. He was also thickly layered in muscle. Rumors had reached Tico that Remus had exploded the heart, pancreas, and one of the lungs of the last person who stood in the ring with him.

Remus didn't stand a chance.

Prizefighting was illegal on Sambala, just as it was everywhere else. Adults who pitted themselves against each other for money or any other reward were punished swiftly and severely.

Unfortunately for Tico, it was not illegal for residents of Sambala to pit their livestock against each other. Livestock were not citizens, so there were no laws being broken.

Not that it mattered.

"Now you go out there and show 'em what you've got." Autis, Tico's owner, a short, pudgy man, had his usual cigar clenched between his teeth. She barely noticed the glowing embers at the end of the thick brown shaft, not that she needed a reminder of what it felt to have the burning cigar-tip pressed against her young flesh.

She would show them, that was certain.

Losing wasn't an option.

Autis had already made it painfully clear what would happen if she lost another match. Her ribs still ached where he had broken them, and she had spent months learning how to walk without a limp. Today's fight was her return bout, the first match she had been in since her loss. If Remus saw her limping into the ring, he would capitalize on the weak point immediately and she would have no chance of survival.

The cheers in the distance rose, and she knew that there was only a matter of minutes before she would be called out to take her place in the ring. She took a deep breath, mentally steeling herself for what was about to happen.

Minutes before she would defend her life.

She exhaled slowly through her teeth, her face a grimace of wrath and eagerness that was more for show than for anything more. She didn't care who won the match, wasn't particularly interested in fighting, but she had no choice. Her fate had long since been decided for her. She had been born to be cattle, as she assumed her parents had been before her, not that she had ever met them or been told anything about who they had been. She lived in this ring, sharing moments of pure violence with whoever entered with her. She would die in this ring; of that, she was sure.

Just not today.

The announcer began to speak. Although she couldn't hear what he was saying over the roaring crowd, it didn't matter. It was always the same. She would be announced first, because officially she was the challenger. Remus would enter after her to defend his position.

"You win this match," Autis spoke quietly into her ear, just loudly enough to be heard over the din, "and you can sleep in the house tonight." It was well into the depths of winter, so the appeal of sleeping in a nice, warm house instead of out in the barn with the rest of his fighting cattle was appealing.

"But if you lose," his grip on her arm tightened, pressing into the fracture point that had only recently healed. She had long ago taught herself how to ignore the pain, showing no sign that she even felt him. "I will kill you myself."

She knew that she had won tons of money for him. He was a very wealthy man, in no small part due to her. Although she couldn't read the contracts he signed every time he entered her into another match, she had overheard plenty of times where the prize amounts were announced. They had started out small, but as she proved herself the amounts increased. Twenty credits, a hundred credits, a thousand credits, tens of thousands of credits. She had lost count of how much she had won for him.

Tonight's match, she knew, was for a million.

His threat was genuine, of that she had no doubts. She wasn't the first prize-fighter he had purchased, and she wouldn't be the last. Just the week before, he had come into the barn and pulled Marco, one of his older boys, out of his stable.

He had lost a thousand-credit match.

She could still hear Marco's screams as Autis had beaten him to death. It hadn't been a swift death; the sun moved from high above the horizon to just below it before Marco fell silent. For encouragement for the rest of his cattle, Autis had left the boy's corpse on the ground just outside the barn.

When Autis had come to fetch her that morning to prepare for that night's bout, she had walked directly past the almost-unrecognizable corpse, which had frozen to the ground during the overnight freeze. A light dusting of snow, far less than was usual for that time of year, covered him in a wintry blanket of crimson.

Tico hardly noticed that she was walking down the long, dim tunnel that led to the arena. As she walked, she tried not to hear what the announcer was saying. She paid no attention to the roar of the crowd, the blinding spotlight that fell on her as she walked into the arena. She listened to her breathing, her footsteps slow and steady as she inhaled and exhaled.

It was a wide, scuffed circle of dirt surrounded by high concrete walls, almost as tall as her cattle barn. The ground hadn't been smoothed since the last battle, so it was scuffed and pitted with splotches of blood and who knew what else everywhere. As she looked around the ground, Tico realized that the last fight in the arena had not been one-on-one, as most of her battles were, but had instead been a team fight. At least three people per team, she thought. Briefly, she wondered whether she would be pitted against more people than she had originally expected.

Not that it mattered.

Above the three-unit-high walls surrounding the arena, rows and rows of seats were filled to bursting with men and women, as well as a few children. Some were dressed in regular workwear, but others had obviously dressed as though it was a special occasion. Formal wear was dotted throughout the box seats, special areas that were reserved for the highest class of attendees. This fight had been highly publicized, then, so everyone had come out to enjoy the sport.

No wonder. It was for a million-credit prize.

Not that it mattered.

Remus entered only a moment later, through an identical tunnel on the other end of the arena. He was tall; over a unit and a half, and his chest, shoulders, and arms were thickly padded with muscle – far too much for him to have built naturally.

His pale blond hair had been cropped short, as had her own. Long hair only got into the way and gave the opponent a way to control you. Tico had cut hers off herself. She was just relieved to see that she had only one opponent. There had been stories of single fighters being put up against impossible odds, two or more on a single person. She figured that if she had to, she could take on two opponents, but if she faced three or more, it might be a bit of a challenge.

Once the announcer finished introducing Remus, the lights dimmed but for the ones directly over the arena. The starting gong sounded and Tico and Remus began to circle the ring, eyeing one another and trying to find the weak spots.

She already knew that he didn't have any, just as she knew that he would go for her eyes.

Everyone did.

Not that it mattered.

With a primal scream, the boy launched across the arena at her. Just as she had predicted, he held both hands out front as he went in for her eyes. He moved a bit faster than she had expected, so she barely had enough time to move away from his lightning-fast attack before he made contact with skin, but she didn't need to move far. She grabbed his outstretched left arm with her left hand as he reached for her, and her fingers dug into his flesh as she pulled him down, pressing against his shoulder with her right hand and using her lower center of gravity to push him off balance. Almost every opponent Tico had been up against had been larger than her, with the odds in their favor because of her minuscule size, particularly when compared against their bulk.

She had learned quickly that there was a substantial benefit to being small.

Apparently aware of that particular maneuver, Remus stepped forward and managed to get his arm out of her grip, turning to face her once more. He tried to dive low, countering her height, but she didn't care. She grabbed him by his shoulder and used his own momentum to pull him forward, stepping lightly out of the way as she pushed him to the ground. As he fell, he ducked his own head and shoulders, turning her maneuver into a forward roll and kicking his feet towards her as he completed his circuit. By shifting her weight, she easily avoided his foot, but his roll forced her to release her grip on his shoulder.

As they squared off again, both having now tested the reflexes of the other, it was obvious who would emerge victorious. While it may not have been apparent to the shouting spectators, resignation already shone in his eyes as he knew the match was lost. That recognition didn't stop him from coming in for another attack, however, this time feinting with his arms and sweeping at her legs with his own feet. Tico had proven too agile to take out head-on as he had originally attempted.

That, too, she had expected.

She tangled his foot with her own, wrapping her heel behind his knee and yanking his leg painfully forward. The crowd screamed again as she placed a hand on the back of his head and thrust his forehead into his own knee. That particular maneuver was dizzying and disorienting, she knew from experience, so she recognized the value of using it against such a large opponent. Blood began to pour from his nose, which had impacted at the same time as his forehead and now sat at an uncomfortable and unnatural angle.

Autis could now accept the prize for her having drawn first blood, one of his particular favorite bets.

Without releasing either his leg or his head, she hopped back-wards on her free foot, pulling Remus sideways as she went. He flopped helplessly onto the ground, barely able to stabilize his fall with one arm as he went. Just before he landed, she unhooked her foot from him and twisted her body, using the now-freed heel to contact his face again as he lifted his head. More blood speckled the arena, now coming from his nose, lower lip, and now his left eye socket.

As he rolled to his back, he made the critical mistake of lifting his hands to his face in an attempt to wipe the blood away so he could see. It was all the opening she needed.

Not that it mattered.

She jumped into the air, lifting her feet high behind her and angling her upper body towards him. She landed exactly as she had expected, and he uncovered his face just in time to witness her elbow make contact with his body. What little weight she held in her tiny body was multiplied by the jump, so that all of the force she could possibly muster was focused on the single sharp point of her elbow, and his sternum was unable to hold up against it.

The fight was over before it really started, in her opinion. She had won, and it had only been a matter of seconds. If the match had lasted more than a minute from the starting gong to the ending gong, she would have been surprised.

Without making a sound, she stood and walked toward her tunnel.

"Kill him," an unidentifiably feminine voice called out from the crowd. "He's not dead yet."

Other voices joined the first and Tico stopped in confusion halfway out of the arena. She had won the fight; there was no way that Remus could get back up to fight her. In fact, she doubted that he would ever get up again, no matter what she did.

This fight, and Remus's fighting days were over, so Autis should already be collecting his prizes for the match settlement.

As she thought, she realized what the call from the crowd meant.

She hadn't been told that this was a death match.

Not that it mattered.

Even more voices joined the chorus, and she turned back to the defeated boy. She looked down at him and watched him heave for breath, no easy feat with as many broken ribs as he had. His eyes were closed, and tears ran freely down his cheeks, coursing through the blood that continued to flow from his ravaged face. She wondered, as she did after many fights, whether he was in some way related to her, if he was born of the same breeding stock as she herself had been. His eyes were both the size of a standard human rather than the oversized ones she herself possessed, which meant that the chances of him being a relative were slight, but that barely mattered. In a way, they were all kin, they were all the same regardless of whom claimed ownership.

She squatted down next to him and looked at him more closely. Pain could cause tears, she knew that from experience, but somehow his were different. His situation was certainly no different from hers, just different owner, different barn and different cattle with whom he would be housed. There would be no sleeping in the warmth of the house for him that night, if that had even been offered to him, and the winter air would certainly bring his young life to an end within a day or two.

"Kill me," he whispered, his voice barely audible over the chanting of the crowd. "If you don't, he will." Despite his brawn, his voice revealed his youth, the small voice of the small child he truly was.

Tico stood back up and surveyed the crowd from her full height. She had no idea who Remus belonged to, but she understood what he had meant. The death that she could give him would be merciful compared to whatever punishment awaited him once he was returned to his owner.

Blinking back tears of sympathy, she raised her foot for the death blow.

SURVIVAL INSTINCTS

The Queen of Diamonds watched as the gun moved, as though everything was in slow motion, and pointed at her head. The barrel looked to be as wide as the hallway, although she knew it to only be as wide as one of her fingers. She felt, rather than saw, everyone around her move aside as the man aimed so that they were all quickly pressed against the corridor walls on either side of her.

The Nine of Clubs had moved as well, positioning herself against the door to keep anyone from following them into the corridor. Although the door was bolted, it was obvious she didn't trust the people on the other side to be keyless. Two men were ahead of Diamond on her left, one with diamond shaped crystals on his lapel and the other with ones shaped like hearts, both bringing weapons similar to the first man's Gasjet to bear. Another man, this one with spade insignia, was ahead on her right and apparently unarmed.

The gunman was almost directly in front of Diamond, less than a unit away, a perfect distance for a point-bank shot. As the barrel rose, Diamond let her vision fade so that all of her attackers but for the Nine of Clubs would be in her peripheral vision. Her normally bright eyes dulled as she expanded her focus.

Her terrified heartbeat slowed to an unnatural calm.

This match was against five people, more than she had ever faced at once in her lifetime.

Not that it mattered.

This match was for her life. That was the only prize, and it was hers alone to claim.

She no longer wore filthy green trunks, having replaced them with a stylish skirt that showcased the length of her legs. Her feet were no longer bare, now supported by tenth-unit heels. Her fingers, no longer calloused and bruised, were smooth and tipped with gleaming red polish. She had no tape to wrap around her hand.

Despite all of the changes, each part of her body remembered what to do. There was no plan; she didn't need one. Muscles moving in accord with memories that had been developed a lifetime ago, she stepped forward, grabbed the gunman's wrist tightly against the handle of the gun, and ducked under his arm as the first shot tore from the barrel. The bullet screamed, echoing in the confined space as it bounced from the metal walls, but she paid it no attention. It was no threat to her. She twisted his arm so that his weapon was aimed at the person standing closest on her left and maneuvered her fingers to squeeze the trigger again.

Blood exploded from his face, painting the walls in a gruesome canvas of death. He didn't get a chance to draw his weapon completely from the holster beneath his coat before falling to the ground, lifeless.

Four.

Diamond didn't stop to consider the ramifications of what she had just done, the life she had taken. She ignored the fact that she had sworn years before to never take another life, human or otherwise. Instead, she continued her momentum, firing the assassin's gun again, the round imbedding itself into the wall just shy of the second man on the left.

The sound of the gunfire was deafening and the thought crossed her mind of how irresponsible the assassin was; he really should have used a silencer. Everyone on the base would know that shots had been fired, and there was likely at least one person on his way to intervene already.

Not that it mattered.

As she spun, she caught the motion of the Nine of Clubs, whose gun was free of her holster as well.

More shots screamed down the corridor towards her and Diamond jerked the assassin by the arm that she held twisted behind his back so that he was between her and the Nine. His body jerked once, twice, three times in rapid succession as Nine's rounds slammed into the impromptu human shield. He slumped against her immediately, his breath rattling out from his lungs one final time before falling silent.

Three.

She released him and his body slumped to the ground as she grabbed the second man, who had only missed being shot seconds earlier, and yanked him in front of her to act as a replacement shield. This assailant had a gun already, but when facing away from her, given her small size against his back, there was no way for him to hit her, except perhaps with a ricochet from one of the walls. That was a risk she was willing to take, as she was just as likely to take such a round from his gun as from the weapons everyone else seemed all too happy to continue firing.

Two.

Thundering sounds emanated from the bolted door as people on the other side, locked away from the carnage, tried to force it open. Diamond knew that Knave was the source, just as well as she knew that there was no way for him to arrive in time to do anything to help her current situation. Even the strength of an angry Tet was not enough to break solid steel walls that quickly.

More rounds flew down the corridor, pounding into her fresh, new replacement body shield until there was a slight lull in the projectile assault. She took the opportunity to duck a shoulder and flip him backwards, using her lowered center of balance and the unnaturally backwards direction to fling him into the final man in the corridor, who had finally drawn his weapon.

One.

Pity. Had he refrained from drawing his gun and pointing it at her as though he actually meant to shoot her, she probably would have let him live.

Not that it mattered. There was only one prize that she cared to claim, the prize of her own life.

Instinct, more powerful than any training she could have ever had, caused her to duck, sensing more than seeing that the Nine had her weapon pointed dangerously close to Diamond's head. She did the only thing she could: She ducked a shoulder, rolled over the dead man on the ground in front of her, and felt a searing flash of pain enter her shoulder and travel all the way to hell and back.

Forcing the pain away, exactly the same as she had done countless times in the arena all those years ago, she sprang up with all the strength she had left in her, leading with her fist. She knew exactly where she was even in the disorienting space and while slipping on the still-warm blood that continued to ooze from the dead man's body. She knew that the rolling maneuver she had done would make her a perfect target for another barrage of bullets but, more importantly, she knew one more thing: she knew where the Nine was.

Whether by accident or design, her clenched fist connected with the soft neck that Nine had left woefully exposed, so certain she had been of her own victory. The woman fired again, but her body was already starting to slump, her windpipe crushed beneath the devastating blow.

"If you can't breathe," Autis's voice echoed from somewhere small and locked away in the back of her memory, not quite as forgotten as she would like it to have been, "you can't fight." The voice, that most hated voice, continued to haunt her even all these years after his death.

Not willing to take any chances, Diamond followed her momentum with an elbow to the front of the woman's face. Not done yet, Diamond reached around Nine's head, grabbed her chin, and twisted with the last of her waning strength.

Bones snapped like breaking twigs and both the Nine and Diamond slumped to the ground at the same time. The last thing she remembered was her hope that it had been enough.

She would know one way or the other, depending on whether she woke back up ever again.

Not that it mattered.

BROKEN PROMISE

When the door to the meeting room burst open, the Knave of Spades identified three assailants, and swift action from both him and the Ten of Clubs dispatched the trio with little effort. As he looked down at the prone figures crumpled in terror on the floor beneath the meeting table, he realized that his initial fear of an assassination attempt on himself and Diamond by Aces couldn't have been true; trained killers wouldn't have gone down that easily.

Instead, he rationalized, they had to be cards who were acting on their own for whatever reason.

Screaming from the shocked cards reverberated throughout the chamber, their sounds echoing in his ears. Some called to each other, checking to ensure everyone was okay. After only a moment, everyone appeared to be safe and whole, now that the threat had been dispersed. The only person who appeared to have been hit in the attack had been the Dolrathi, who insisted it was a minor wound at most.

The chaos in the meeting room had subsided almost as swiftly as it began, and as people climbed back to their feet, it had taken another second and a half to realize that Diamond was missing.

He looked around, trying to figure out where she had hidden herself so that he could reassure her she was safe when he heard the unmistakable thud as the heavy bolt on the airlock door that led to the maintenance corridor at the back end of the room slide home. A second glance told him all that he needed to know.

The Nine of Clubs was missing.

He tore a piece of paper out of his pocket and threw it at the Ten of Spades. "Get these people here now," he bellowed as he sprang for the door.

Gunshots echoed from the far side of the wall once, twice, a hundred times as he slammed his shoulder against the secured door. He knew what to expect from his actions. He had specifically ordered every unit of material on that base and knew what it would take to make it through the door once it was sealed. Rationality had nothing to do with it, however, and he continued to shove with all of his might.

It didn't budge.

Terror struck cold shards of ice through the Knave of Spades's heart as the thunder of gunfire, barely muffled by the reinforced steel, stopped. He slammed his shoulder into the door again, calling upon his entire lineage to give him strength now that he desperately needed it, and then impacted the door a third time before he felt it begin to give way. Three more hard impacts removed the door almost entirely from its hinges in a shriek of torn metal. It swung into the corridor, only stopping from falling completely to the ground by the lowermost hinge, which had still refused to give way.

Carnage greeted him on the other side.

The first thing he caught sight of was a crumpled, destroyed body slumped against the wall of the corridor, its head hanging at an unnatural angle and a mess of bloody pulp where the face was supposed to be. The only recognizable portion of the Nine of Spades was her long auburn hair, matted and stained with her own blood.

Four more men lay in assorted states of dead, most peppered with bullet holes. Blood continued to spread across the floor as the last traces of life leaked from them, making the entire surface of the corridor slick and virtually impossible to maneuver on.

Next to the Nine of Clubs lay a small form, motionless. She was covered in even more blood than any of the dead men in the hall, and almost as much as Nine. "Oh, no," he moaned as he slipped his way to her. Beneath all the blood, she had almost no color.

Her pulse was weak but present, and he gently picked her up, lifting her from the grotesque display, and carried her out into the meeting room.

The Ten of Spades had sent people out to find the people on his list remarkably quickly, and all of them were in the process of gathering in the meeting room. Everyone's eyes widened as they saw the motionless form of the Queen of Diamonds as Knave gently placed her on one of the tables to examine her injuries. Hushed whispers and quiet conversations filled the room as everyone wondered whether their leader was dead.

"Sir," the Tet asked hesitantly as he stepped up next to Knave. "I got almost all of the people you requested."

"Almost?"

"Yes. The Nine of Clubs is missing."

"Arrest them," Knave growled in response. He didn't look up from his examination of Diamond.

"Sir?"

"I said arrest them!" Knave shouted to the stunned room, the loudest any of them had ever heard from him, and with all the fury of the Tet he truly was. "Every single one of the people on that list is a spy for the King of Clubs. They are all equally responsible for this," he gestured towards the motionless figure on the table, "and I want them in shackles *right now*!"

Without hesitation, the eleven people that had been brought at his orders were stripped of their weapons, knocked to the ground, and thoroughly bound hand and foot. Some of the cards looked dazed as they secured their comrades, but they did as he had instructed without argument.

The infiltrators had done their job far too well, Knave realized. Diamond's hopes that the Ten would have identified them as spies had been in vain and he bit back a bout of self-derision, knowing that he should have pushed the issue of their removal far sooner. Even those who lived with them, who worked with them every day and who now arrested them hadn't recognized them for what they truly were.

"What shall we do with them?" Ten inquired.

"Put them on my ship," Knave said without looking up from Diamond's bleeding wounds. "And someone give me a hand with her."

"Is she still alive?" Ten asked as he moved around the low table to help him move Diamond.

"For now," Knave nodded. "But she won't be for long if I don't get her to a doctor, quickly." With Ten's assistance, he moved Diamond, still on top of the table, onto the ship. Although Knave was worried about how well she would travel on the flat surface, it was a far better option than moving her around too much by carrying her by herself. The risk of doing additional damage to her while trying to save her weighed heavily on his mind.

The spies that Knave had ordered arrested were loaded into one of the ship's cargo holds, the door securely barred behind them. Knave didn't care that it was about to get very cold in the cargo hold, as their comfort barely even registered on his current list of concerns.

"I'll contact you soon," Knave promised as they set the table down. "Just keep everyone doing what they were doing until then."

"Where are you taking her?" Ten asked as Knave secured Diamond for flight. His brows were creased with worry – the genuine kind, not the false concern of a spy.

"Her shoulder blade's broken," Knave explained. "I can't tell how much internal damage there is. But there's only one place I know of that can take care of injuries this severe."

"You mean..." Ten's voice was quiet with surprise. "You're taking her to Lovus?"

"That's right," Knave agreed as he held the door for the leader of the Ghiel base. "We're going to Midway General."

MIDWAY GENERAL

When Diamond regained consciousness, she couldn't imme-diately identify where she was. She found herself in a dimly-lit room, on a moderately hard bed and covered by a thin, cream-colored blanket. Blue lights flickered and traced lines on a pair of monitors next to the bed and an assortment of tubes and wires connected the monitors to Diamond's arm.

A thin blue screen, held to the ceiling by a series of rollers on a curved track, blocked her from seeing anything past the bed she lay on and a few square units of space surrounding it. The material wasn't very thick, she realized, but no shadows played across it, so there couldn't be much more illumination on the other side of the movable wall than there was on her side.

Voices, low and calm, flickered past, growing and fading as the speakers passed. Most of the voices spoke in Commish, which was no surprise as Commish was the dominant language used throughout the galaxy. Occasionally, however, smatterings of Dol-rathi, Ruathan, and even Lovan reached her ears and at the sound of the latter, her eyes widened in surprise. The only places where

Lovan was commonly used were on Lovus itself or wherever large portions of Triad's army were stationed.

She looked at the wires in horror, wondering what kind of vile experiments were being performed on her while she was kept asleep. In a panic, she began to tear the tubes from her skin, pulling a long, thin needle out of her arm in the process. Blood flowed from the wound where the needle had been inserted, but she didn't care.

As she ripped at the lines, alarms began to sound from the monitors and she knew that she didn't have much time before her captors discovered she was awake. Still not comprehending where she was or how she had gotten into this predicament, she didn't want to be rendered unconscious again. Unconscious people had no control at all over what happened to them while they slept.

Whimpering softly to herself, not bothering to keep her *tress* or the emotions that caused their display under control, she tugged the last of the attachments free and slipped to the floor. The linoleum underfoot was cold and smooth, but she barely noticed. Nor did she pay any attention to the slow dripping of fluids nearby.

A door on the far side of the room opened and people began rushing in towards her. A cacophony of noise and lights assaulted her senses, disorienting her further, and she reached for the first weapon she could put her hands on. She could barely see with the sudden change of brightness, but that didn't matter. Vision was only one sense and she had plenty more upon which she could rely.

A tall thin metal pole, dangling with a trio of plastic bags that had been holding the poisons going into her arm, was directly next to her. Ignoring the vile fluids that were now freely leaking across the floor, she picked up the metal hanger and swung it with all of her strength at the first person who got close enough to strike. The bags flew free, dropping with a series of thumps onto the floor nearby, but she paid them no attention.

Three people, all dressed in identical powdery-blue uniforms and faces covered in cloth masks, fell beneath her defense before another person came running into the room. This person, dressed differently than all the others and face uncovered, jumped over the bed to land directly in front of her. He only grunted as she slammed the metal pole, which was already badly bent, across his midsection.

As she pulled back to take another swing at this latest intruder, she looked upwards to his face in order to strike a critical blow but stopped and blinked in surprise. She recognized those eyes – all three of them. "Knave?" she asked, her voice hoarse and dry.

He reached out for her, wrapping one arm around her shoulder and gently taking the bar from her hands with the other. "It's okay," he reassured her as he set the mangled bar onto the bed. "You're safe now."

More people scrambled into the room, but Diamond refused to let go of her friend, refused to even acknowledge that the others were there. "Where are we?" she asked as the terror began to fade. "What are they doing to us?"

"We're at the hospital," he explained as he lifted her onto the bed, shoving her makeshift weapon to the opposite side of the floor in the process. "You're safe now but you were hurt pretty badly."

Flashes of the assault on Ghiel flickered in her memory but refused to take hold, causing her to groan and drop her head into her hands in pain. "I was..." she tried to fight through the pain, which had started to spread out to more than just her head. Her arms ached, especially where she had ripped the needle from her skin. Dark liquid dripped down her forearm and she wondered whether it was blood or one of the fluids that had been in the plastic bags.

Her legs hurt, too, as though she had pulled every muscle in them. A thousand tiny pains brought her attention to exactly where the wires had been attached to her body, but most of all her back and one of her shoulders burned with white-hot fire.

"You were attacked," he explained. "You got hurt pretty badly so I brought you here to get put back together."

"Here..." She looked around again and realized that, far from the torture chamber she had initially believed herself to be in, she was in a hospital room. "Where is here?"

"Midway General," a voice that wasn't Knave's answered. "You've been here for almost a month."

She looked up, startled. Standing next to the bed, on the opposite side as Knave, was a man who appeared to be just beginning his middle years. He had light brown hair, concerned hazel eyes, and shoulders wide enough to land a shuttle on. As she watched, he bent down to retrieve the IV pole that she had destroyed, handing it to one of the orderlies who waited just beyond the curtain and well outside of her reach.

"A month?" She looked from the doctor to Knave, who nodded in agreement.

"Closer to three weeks than a month, but you've been here for a while," he confirmed.

She shook her head slowly, trying to arrange the chaotic jumble of thoughts into a recognizable pattern. "A month," she muttered. "Midway General. I was attacked."

In a rush, it came flooding back to her. She remembered the assault on Ghiel, the betrayal and attempted assassination by the Nine of Clubs and her friends, but nothing afterwards. Her eyes flew open in shock as Knave's statement registered and she reached for her friend's hand. "Midway General!" She turned to meet his gaze. "I'm on Lovus?"

She didn't have to explain the raw fear to him, he already understood. "Everything's fine," he reassured her. "Like I said, you're safe." He lowered his voice. "Just try not to talk too much, okay?"

She blinked at him and nodded.

The doctor, whose name badge read *Goober*, which was more likely to be a nickname than a real one, cautiously reached out a hand toward her, careful to keep it where she could see it. "We need to check on a couple things," he explained as he gently pressed her back onto the mattress. His touch wasn't rough, it was soothing, as a doctor's hands should be. "It looks like you've healed well, but we need to make sure that you'll continue to improve."

She nodded wordlessly at the doctor, keeping an attentive eye on exactly what he was doing. Although she didn't reveal anything, part of her attention was directed at the others in the room, who were doctors and orderlies if she had to guess. For the most part, the assembled crowd seemed more concerned with getting the people she had wounded out of the room and getting themselves out of harm's way as well, which was good riddance as far as she was concerned. The fewer people in the room, the less she had to worry about.

Dr. Goober checked her breathing and heart rate, as she had expected, before pressing his fingers in a circular pattern around her stomach. "Everything still seems to be where it belongs," he said after examining her for about five minutes.

He helped her lean forward again so that he could check on her back. She hissed in pain when he pressed against her shoulder blade, and he pursed his lips at the noise. It hadn't bothered her while she had been in the grips of panic but, now that she was substantially calmer, she realized that she must have taken a significant amount of damage in order for it to hurt so much. Either that, she realized, or she had pulled a muscle by exerting herself so much after almost a month of inactivity. Neither option gave her comfort.

The doctor was quick to describe the source of her pain. "Your scapula was almost completely destroyed," he explained as he helped her lay flat again. "We regenerated most of it, but it's still going to be sore for a while. It's a large chunk of bone, and it's still knitting itself together.

"The internal damage seems to have healed almost completely. Your lungs have full pressure again and the bullet and bone shards didn't puncture anything else vital."

He pulled a chart from the foot of her bed, pulled a pen out of his jacket pocket, and made a couple of notes inside. "Like I said, your bones, including your scapula, aren't quite finished healing, though," he explained as he dropped her file back into its holder, "so you'll need to be careful of them for the next six weeks or so. No strenuous exercise, and definitely no more beating up on my nursing staff, got it?" The twinkle in his eye showed that he wasn't as upset by her actions as his words made it seem.

She nodded, grateful that he hadn't asked how the bones had gotten broken in the first place, or from where the bullets he had removed had come, because she wasn't sure how to answer those types of questions yet. From the lack of scrutiny in Dr. Goober's expression, however, she assumed that Knave had made some sort of plausible excuse for them both.

Nor did he ask about any of her older, long-since-healed wounds. She had even less of an idea of how to explain those, so she hoped he hadn't uncovered them but quickly sent that hope away. The doctors in Midway General were the best in the galaxy so if there were injuries to be found, they had found them.

"When can I be released?" she asked, trying to keep the fear out of her voice. Midway General was the largest, most well-equipped hospital on Lovus, mostly because it was the hospital where Triad sent their troops when they were injured. The last thing she needed was for someone to discover who she was and turn her in. Although she didn't follow such news, she knew that there was an impressive bounty on her capture and there were plenty of people who might be interested in becoming rich.

"Probably in a few more days," Goober answered after a moment's thought. "Since you're awake, most of the danger's already passed. But we'll want to keep an eye on you for a little while, just to be sure you don't overtax that new bone structure of yours, and to make sure there aren't any other problems popping up once you're mobile."

She nodded quietly. A few days she could handle. After all, hadn't she already been there for almost a month?

The last place she had wanted to find herself was on Lovus, specifically because of her current wanted status and the proximity to Triad's troops should they discover she was there. As soon as the doctor left, she turned to Knave.

"Are they really just going to let us go in a few days?" she asked in amazement.

He nodded and smiled down at her. "Triad knows about the coup," he reminded her. "Seems to me that, although they can't outright encourage what we've been doing, they seem to be willing to look the other way, at the very least."

"But how can we be sure?" she wanted to know. "What if they're just waiting for me to be healthy enough to go to jail?"

He sighed and reached for the file at the end of her bed, the same one in which Goober had been taking notes during his examination. "Lovan bio scanners are sensitive enough to track everything about a patient from the DNA out, right?" When she nodded, he continued. "Because of that, it's impossible to trick them by using a false name, right?" When she agreed again, he dropped the folder onto her lap.

"That says your name is Michelle Deva," he pointed out. "We both know that's not even close to the truth."

"But..." she looked from the name on the folder to him, realization dawning on her. "They can't be fooled," she said in wonder, "but as long as they have a reasonable excuse, they can look the other way."

He nodded and smiled, and she looked back down at the papers thoughtfully. She wasn't enthused about seeing the name, one she expected to have left behind on Earth, but if that was all she had to agree to in order to walk out of the medical center belonging to the strongest military force in the galaxy, it was a small price to pay.

After all, it would hardly be the first time she had needed to go by a false name.

"Remind me later to send Commander Moore another gift basket. And see if you can find more star-fruit in the meantime."

Four days later, Goober and his team determined that the patient they knew as Michelle Deva was well enough to travel. She and Knave returned to their personal base on Terros so that she could continue to recuperate in relative peace, without looking over her shoulder every few seconds, checking to see if an arrest team had arrived for her. She could hardly believe that she had been to Lovus, nor that she had been allowed to simply leave as soon as their business, and her treatment, was complete.

As much as she wanted to stop in at Ghiel and Majapa to see how things had been going in her absence, as well as to reassure them that she wasn't dead, she just didn't want to deal with any of the people yet.

For right now, she thought to herself, *I need peace and quiet to think.*

CHAPTER

28

BRINGING THE BATTLE TO THEM

Diamond's *tress* blazed a bright, violent red. It had begun to flare while she was still in the hospital, and the recuperation time Knave insisted she take at Terros hadn't helped calm them in the slightest.

Outwardly, she gave no indication of the wrath she felt inside. She had thought that she'd felt anger before but, when compared to the torrent of fury that burned within her, what she had felt previously had been nothing more than irritation, like the sting of a bee on the sole of her foot or running out of honey to sweeten her tea.

She wanted, more than anything else, to let the King of Clubs know that he wouldn't be allowed to get away with a stunt like what had been pulled on Ghiel. She wanted to make him and all who remained loyal to him feel their mistake to the last man.

Against half a lifetime of passive nonviolence, the revenge her soul demanded weighed heavily.

The worst part, she realized, was that she couldn't exact her retribution against the individual cards who had attempted to kill her. They had already paid, appropriately and definitively, for that crime. She had exacted the payment herself. The other traitors on the Ghiel base, ones who hadn't been involved in the actual assault, had been turned over to Triad to face justice from them.

Or at least, she realized, that was what she had been told. When the thought flickered through her mind that there was no way to keep the traitorous cards from informing Triad about their lunar base, the obvious answer came to her immediately. Rather than inquiring about it, however, she chose to remain in silent ignorance on that particular topic.

It wasn't even that she had suddenly become bloodthirsty, either. The deaths that she had brought with her own hands, no matter how justified, kept her from sleeping comfortably at night. The blood, the broken bones, the silent agony of those lives she had taken haunted her dreams. Not just those whose lives she had taken during the assault, but plenty more that she had taken a lifetime ago.

The cards who had attempted to assassinate her on Ghiel weren't the only faces haunting her. Remus, her first kill, who had begged her for merciful death at the conclusion of her very first death match, had been a constant nocturnal companion for years. Others tormented her as well; boys and girls, both younger than she and older.

She had no idea, no clue whatsoever about how many people she had killed in her life, but if the ghostly images that visited her every night were any indication, they numbered in the thousands.

Still, she pushed the ghosts aside to focus on the more current problem at hand; she needed to find a way to send a message to all of the King of Clubs' cards. One that wasn't too violent – the fewer corpses added to those already accumulated on her conscience, the better – but one that was strong enough for every member of the Deck to hear and understand.

"There are some good things happening, too," Knave said in an attempt to cheer her as he handed her a fresh cup of tea. "I've kept in contact with the leaders of all three bases and they all report no problems with the operations already in place." She had forgotten until that statement that she had authorized the expansion into Ziloc only hours before her encounter on Ghiel. In her absence, Knave and the Ten had overseen the entire operation.

It was a meager ray of hope in the bitter darkness, but Diamond was willing to accept Knave's attempt to cheer her. "How are things at the crystal mines going?"

"Completely under control," he answered proudly.

She scowled at him. "We already know that," she snapped. "What about production? What about distribution? Do we have buyers for any of the crystal, or are we just selling on the open market?"

"Production hasn't changed; it's the same as it was before we took over. Part of the crystal is available on the open market, but that's mostly the smaller stuff. The larger pieces are either being offered to some of our regular buyers or used to entice new ones to do business with us."

"What kind of new buyers?"

"World Industries," he explained, beaming.

His pride was earned, she had to admit. She had been trying since her return to generate new contacts within the manufacturing company, with very little success. Since World Industries was responsible for the manufacture of so many different types of vehicles, many of which required large quantities of pure crystals, his news of developing such a contact and beginning a new trade relationship was both welcome and impressive.

Diamond took a deep, calming breath. She hadn't meant to snap at her friend like that, and she had known before asking that the mines would be running smoothly. "Sorry," she mumbled as she took a sip of the sweet jasmine-scented beverage.

"Don't worry about it," he brushed her apology aside just as he had her anger. "The palladium mines, on the other hand, have finally started to produce."

"About time," she growled into the cup. "Our predictions showed that it would only take a month to get those up and running again. What took so long?"

"The usurper's Deck," he answered. "Apparently, they weren't amused about our positioning in the Ravenstar system. They sent troops in to try and roust us, but we drove them off."

She winced. If the King of Clubs had sent troops to drive them away from Tegintys, there had likely been even more bloodshed than what she had already suspected while she had been out of commission.

As if reading her thoughts, he reassured her, "Most of the people they sent voluntarily defected to our side, so the damage wasn't that bad, overall." Before she could object, he added, "I had them confirmed by Protus. A handful of them have already been turned over to Triad, and the rest are on Mota."

"Speaking of Triad," he changed the subject, "Commander Moore called earlier. He wants to thank you for the fruit basket and to know whether you plan to return Goober's identification card or if the hospital needs to issue him a replacement."

"He can have it back," she sighed, "if he really needs it."

Knave raised his central eyebrow. "You sure?" he asked. "Normally when you take stuff like that you keep it as a trophy." He gestured towards her stands of similar trophies on display, trophies she hadn't added to since their first day back on Terros.

"No," she slowly shook her head and took another sip of her tea. "It was a stupid thing to take. I'll call Moore and let him know that we'll drop it off with the next delivery." She realized that the tea wasn't quite as sweet as she would have preferred and stood to head for the kitchen. It was a new blend, she recognized, so of course Knave wouldn't know how sweet she would want it.

"Activity in the Oberron system seems to be picking up," he called after her as she walked out of the room. As a direct result of the increased troops the King of Clubs had sent to the Oberron system, Triad finally sent in troops of their own. Shipping lines had been disrupted far more effectively than Diamond had predicted, and the Interplanetary Government was feeling the impact. Even if she hadn't interfered, it was highly likely that Triad would have arrived on scene shortly regardless. The Oberron system was simply too important for them to leave it in the King of Clubs's irresponsible hands.

None of these things mattered, she realized.

The King and his Deck were growing stronger by the day.

She was stirring the honey into her cup of tea when an idea struck her. She dropped the spoon in surprise as everything became clear. "Knave," she called out. "I have an idea!"

"So do I," he said as he stepped into the room. With how swiftly he entered, he must have been waiting out of sight just beyond the doorway when she had called for him. "I think we can take back Cardiss."

"One thing I discovered," Knave said as he followed her back to the living room. There, he stacked thick files onto the coffee table, the results of his endless research, "is that it may be possible to reverse an EMP blast."

"But EMP weapons are useless," Diamond countered with a single eyebrow raised in confusion. "That's why nobody uses them anymore."

When ships filled with pioneers had first headed out to explore the stars and particularly the planets that orbited them, they hadn't counted on finding out that some of the planets were already inhabited. Fighting over the planets that were not inhabited, with many people believing that the invaders were simply too close to areas they considered to be parts of their own territories, ensued.

Electromagnetic Pulse weapons, better known as EMPs, had been some of the most valuable weapons during the infancy of space travel. By using such weaponry, ships equipped with EMP weapons could knock out the electrical systems of their target without doing physical damage, allowing for the takeover and resulting acquisition to their own forces. This tactic lasted for a great many years, but soon EMP, just as with almost every other form of warfare, became antiquated as better defenses were developed. Soon, because of the devastating effects of EMP weapons, every ship still functioning was fitted with shielding that would disperse the blast and render the energy weapons useless.

"Against anything that has a class three or lower technology level, that's true," he acquiesced. "Shielding against EMP will stop all electronic pulse weapons, but what about a weapon that does the exact opposite?"

She blinked at him in confusion, eyebrow still raised, trying to figure out what he was getting at. "Why would you want to reverse an EMP?" she asked finally. "Wouldn't that do, well, nothing?"

"Not quite," he answered as he pulled a file from the middle of the stack. As he flipped through the pages, he continued. "EMP works by overloading the electrical flow of whatever it's fired at. But I think that by reversing the electronic signature of the weapon, it could slow the electrical system of the target to the point where it shuts down due to lack of power." He pulled a page of notes from the back of the file, a page that had sketches drawn in the margins to match the notes. "Since just about everything has buffers in place to control the power flow from going too high, sending too much energy would be pointless. But if we reverse the flow, that will cause the energy flow to not overload but instead to cease, resulting in a critical shutdown of all systems," he explained further as he set the solitary paper down and smoothed it across the table. "Buffers aren't designed to keep the energy going, they're designed to keep it under a specific level."

"All systems?" Diamond shook her head. "You mean like life support?"

"It's not as bad as you're thinking," he quickly reassured her, understanding immediately where her objections to his plan lie. "True, it would shut down the life support systems, but there will still be enough air left inside for everyone to get to escape ships and safely evacuate."

It really didn't sound too bad, the way he explained it. Compared to some of the weapons that had been used during the heaviest portion of the wars, this sounded practically humane. Diamond had heard of a cyber-weapon known as the Bloodhound Virus that had been used against a mammoth space station, years ago during one of the wars. The attack had opened every airlock on the station, killing almost every person inside instantly. Fewer than two dozen people had managed to get themselves into escape pods before being sucked out into the vacuum of space.

To Diamond's knowledge, that particular attack had only been used once ending the second galaxy-wide war. No further uses had been necessary. She shuddered just thinking about it.

When Knave first started talking about reversing the EMP, she thought he might have been talking about a similar attack. Since his idea allowed enough time for people to escape, however, it didn't violate her nonviolence policy. It could kill people, she recognized, but they would at least have a fighting chance.

It was close, though, which she realized. A year ago, or even just a couple months ago, she would never have agreed to such a maneuver. But with the way she was feeling lately, it seemed almost like a good idea. She briefly wondered whether revenge played a part in her lax feelings towards their discussions on the assault on Cardiss, but while she admitted it probably did, she didn't particularly care.

She wanted her base back.

"This is definitely not as bad as the Bloodhound Virus. I've run thousands of simulations," he explained as she started to cave. "At first it was just for curiosity, but then I started checking to see what the limits of a weapon like that would be."

She cringed at the word weapon, but didn't say no.

"The only real problem I see" he continued, "will be getting it close enough to use. It's got a pretty short effective range, so I'll have to be pretty close up to use it."

"I have an idea on how that could happen," she said. "I was thinking about how, back on Earth, the gnats would flock around you, and no matter how much you swat at them you'd never seem to hit anything."

He chuckled. "I remember. It's almost as though the pesky little things weren't even solid until they landed in your eyes. Wasn't that one of the reasons we moved out of Florida?"

"No, that was because of the mosquitos." She smiled at the memory. "And while I was thinking about some of the places we'd lived on Earth, I started to wonder if there were any copycats of us floating around."

"Probably," he chuckled. "But I'm pretty sure that deVann and his men would have picked off any of them that came on the radar fairly quickly."

"Because they'd spent so much time hunting for us that tracking down someone that wasn't us would be a lot easier."

He looked askance at her. "What are you getting at?"

"We should clone ourselves."

"That's illegal," he answered immediately. Except in extreme cases, which were primarily reserved for the military, cloning had been outlawed across most of the galaxy. Not that it mattered, of course. They both knew that there were pockets where cloning was used regularly.

"Since when does that matter?" she laughed. "But I didn't mean literally."

"Oh." He relaxed considerably at her admission, his eyes slowly widening as he understood where she was heading. "You want to start creating copycats?"

"Exactly," she grinned at him. "If we begin to train some of our people to use the same tactics we use, the King of Clubs and his Aces won't be able to tell the difference."

"You intend for us to use them as a cover while we sneak in with the reverse EMP." His brown eyes flashed with anticipation. "I never really thought I'd get the opportunity to build one. Now we just need to decide on a target."

"Cardiss."

He chuckled for a moment before halting. "You're serious." It wasn't a question, as he noticed she wasn't sharing the joke. "You really want to take Cardiss back?"

"Yes," she answered simply. "I've been trying to decide what I can do, what actions I can take, that would explain to the King of Clubs exactly how serious we are about taking our base back... all of our operation, for that matter."

"But... You said we weren't ready to take the Cardiss base on yet."

"We weren't," she answered calmly, taking another drink of her tea. She leveled her cool green eyes at him. "But now we have enough people, we have enough equipment, and we've got them stretched out thinly enough that we should have a chance."

"I know how badly you want this," he tried to reason with her. He understood how important her organization was to Diamond, as well as how much it galled her to sit back and watch as the King of Clubs continued his campaign of terror and hostility against the galaxy. "But don't you think that it's a bit early? I mean, you just had some pretty major medical work done and it's understandable that you're angry about it..."

She interrupted him before he could continue the thought. "I can't just sit here and do nothing while that idiot and his minions run roughshod over everything." Tears of frustration welled up in her eyes, and for an Emovete, even a part-Emovete like the Queen of Diamonds, that was no small matter.

"I'm not acting irrationally," she defended as she wiped the moisture away. "And this isn't just because of what happened on Ghiel. You and I both know we need to get the base back from them. We've known it the whole time. There's never been a point where taking back Cardiss wasn't part of the plan.

"Now, if we build this reverse EMP of yours and then we swarm the airspace around the base with ships piloted by our people, we've got about as good of a shot, if not better of a shot, as we've ever anticipated of actually getting in." She took a deep breath, trying to calm herself, but her *tress* refused to fade.

"Yes, I'm angry about the attack." Her voice was much more serene than she truly was as she continued. "I'm angry that I didn't recognize the warning signs when we first arrived, and I'm angry that we allowed the Nine of Clubs and her goons to stay on Ghiel in the first place.

"But what I am *not* doing," she leaned forward to emphasize the point, "is letting my anger determine my actions."

He was silent for a long moment after she finished speaking. He looked from her eyes to her shoulder where the bullet had entered, shattering bones along the way. He looked at her *tress*, which were the same vibrant red they had been when she woke in Midway General.

He was trying to think of something, anything, in her body language that would indicate that she had the slightest doubt over whether or not her plan would work, but there was nothing.

"Okay," he acquiesced. "I guess it's time to go home."

CHAPTER

29

POWER SOURCE

Deciding to go home, Diamond decided, was a lot easier than actually *doing* it. She and Knave had increased their recruitment almost immediately and new troops had flocked to their Deck like geese flying south to roost in familiar grounds for the winter. Every day, it seemed, she had another roster of new troops waiting for her, many from units that had recently been under the control of the King of Clubs.

There was no point in even trying to deny that these new recruits were troops. Even the people who were sent out to enroll new members to the Deck called them troops. For some reason, though, it was easier to find people of all races who wanted to fight than it was to find people to be sneaky. Diamond would never understand why people found violence, even the potential for violence, so appealing.

Today's reports were no different. Almost fifty fresh recruits had been delivered to the Mota base and almost all of them had been suited and ranked. They would begin their battle training in the next few days. Far from the scant handful they had started with, her new Deck stood with more manpower than she had ever controlled before. The sheer number of people who now answered to her was almost overwhelming, but she refused to be daunted.

"Hey Diamond," Knave stepped into her office, holding some of his never-ending schematics and simulation reports. "Do you have a couple minutes?"

"Sure." She dropped the latest progress report onto an ever-increasing stack of the same. The reports themselves were purely informational, after all. There was nothing to be done with the files but to set them aside to collect dust. For the first time since she had discovered the world beyond the arena, when she had first learned of Triad and the exalted position within it held by Commander Ryan Moore, she was absolutely devoid of any jealousy. If this nonsense was what he had to deal with every day, then he could just keep it. "What's on your mind?"

Knave had been hard at work on building the reverse EMP for the better part of the last four months while Diamond had worked on building the troops and initiating a training program for them. He had built and discarded more prototypes than Diamond cared to remember, and she winced as she recognized that this looked suspiciously like another prototype down the drain. It was a good thing that their income streams were still going strong, she realized. He was doing a fantastic job of spending all of their credits on supplies for his prototype weapon.

"I hit another glitch," he admitted. "The power supply I was using wasn't powerful enough to generate a strong enough beam to shut down the entire base."

She groaned and dropped her head onto the table. "So, what do you need?" she asked, her voice muffled against the wooden surface.

"You're not going to like it." He had moved closer before answering, so now it sounded like he was standing directly next to her. "The best option I came up with involves a black-hole generator."

She raised her head in surprise, already shaking it vehemently. There was only one system in the galaxy that made and used that type of device, and they had long ago been deemed too dangerous to use elsewhere in the galaxy. Black holes, which generated almost unfathomable amounts of gravity, were perfectly safe while they were under containment, but the concern was that should the containment fail, the result would be an unstoppable force that could destroy anything that came within its range. "No way. The Interplanetary Government's got sniffers out all over the place, keeping an eye out for black holes. If we bring a generator here, it'll bring them down on all of our heads." Diamond herself was not opposed to the use of the controversial machines but the risk was simply too great for this type of operation.

The idea of generating a black hole wasn't completely theoretic. Eighty years ago, the only inhabited planet in the Aminda system had been considered a class four planet because of its lack of space capability. The residents of that planet, named the same as the system it occupied, had rocketed to a class seven in the space of three years when they had harnessed the power of gravity itself to power their new ships.

At first, the black hole-driven craft were unstable and there had been hundreds, thousands of lives lost as the man-made vortices exploded. Three small planets within the Aminda system had been lost and the Interplanetary Government passed swift judgment in the name of galactic security.

Today, the Amindans met with trade ships and other vessels in the narrow buffer zone that had been put into place around their system. None of their ships were allowed to pass into Interplanetary Government space under threat of live fire, despite the advances that the Amindans had made in stabilizing their power systems. No catastrophic failures had been reported in almost fifty years but that wasn't very long in the space-time continuum.

Furthermore, all of their smaller black hole generators were under a strict trade embargo, so anyone caught bringing one across the border was dealt a swift, harsh penalty.

None of this had mattered much to Diamond, who had monitored the activity and progress within the Aminda system as she had everywhere else: with a slight detachment and watching for anything produced within the system that she could profit from.

It wasn't that she refused to do business on Aminda; on the contrary, three of her best buyers lived there, as did one of the finest aerogel manufacturers anywhere. For years, her people had moved into and out of the system on a regular basis, stealing shipments of aerogel and selling them to the highest buyer or delivering purchases made by her buyers. Sometimes, all of these things were accomplished with a single trip.

Be that as it may, she had no intention of bringing anything as controlled and closely monitored as a black hole generator, even a small one. At least, not until she had the time and mental bandwidth to come up with a means by which she could do so without getting caught. She was certain she could, but it would take more planning and time than she had available. "You'll need to come up with a different idea."

"I have." He grinned his slow, sly smile that told her that he had known she would shoot down the idea of smuggling one of the desired generators for him. "The only other option I could come up with is a nuclear reactor."

She blinked at him for a moment in disbelief. "Those things aren't even made anymore," she said. "The only place you could find one is in a junk heap." Many years previously, before humans had even begun exploring the stars, nuclear power had been a big deal. Much of their power had come from nuclear reactors but the residual castoff from such power generation had been radioactive and they had been unable to devise a method by which it could be safely disposed. Even worse but unsurprising given how warlike some of the clans of humans had been in those days, they had discovered how to turn their power source into weapons. Some of the most dangerous physical weaponry developed had involved nuclear devices. As scientific developments had advanced, however, the appeal of nuclear power and weapons had decreased until they became barely more than a footnote in history.

"Nope." His grin widened as he settled into the chair next to her. "Just because we don't use them anymore doesn't mean other people don't."

"But you'd have to go to a class three, maybe class two, planet to find one," she argued. "They're the only ones that use them regularly, but they use them for everything. There's no way you'd be able to just walk in and take one."

"Not on a class two planet," he agreed. "They're too reliant on them."

"But an early class two wouldn't have nuclear yet," she continued, "and a class three would..." Her voice trailed off as she realized where he was leading her in his argument.

"Just be getting away from nuclear power," he agreed. "And we happen to know of one class three planet that still uses a little bit of nuclear, and we happen to know the geography and people rather well."

Her heart sank. "You want to go back to Earth."

"Just for business," he was quick to answer. "I have no intention of getting stuck there again."

His argument was valid, so there was nothing else for her to do but agree. Her plan depended on his reverse EMP, and he couldn't build it unless they went back to Earth.

CHAPTER

30

THE SUBMARINE THIEF

"deVann?" Agent Wick, one of the members of the FBI task force headed by Special Investigator Lucas deVann leaned around the door of his office to peer inside.

"What is it?" deVann asked irritably. He had been put in charge of the task force over ten years ago and, although he had assembled the best team of investigators he could have ever hoped for, they hadn't even come close to the fugitives he had been charged with apprehending.

One wall of his office was covered with an assortment of maps. It had started as just a map of the United States but shortly after beginning his investigation, he had discovered that his targets could operate outside the country as easily as they could inside. He quickly added maps of all the regions the fugitives had been spotted in, expanding his search area every time there was a new report. He still wasn't certain that the pair had actually been to each of the posted countries, but he refused to rule anything out until he was certain one way or another. Now, almost the entire world was depicted on his office wall, with multicolored, flagged tacks stuck into it everywhere the thefts had been reported.

Other papers and notes lined the rest of his walls: memos tacked up here and there, screen grabs of auctions where the authorities had been helpless to stop the sale of one item or another, many of which they didn't even realize had been stolen by the time the sale was complete, and countless photos of authentic pieces of art that had been stolen. In many cases, there was a second photo tacked up next to the first, one which looked almost identical.

Almost. These second pictures were images of the forgeries the thieves had left in place of some of the priceless paintings, sculptures, and other pieces of history they had taken. The forgeries were so good, in fact, that there was still debate in a couple of instances over whether the art on public display was real or fake. Many of the curators of different collections were hesitant at best to say that their valuables had been taken and replaced with forgeries.

deVann knew better. Whether any of the experts the agency had called in to help him identify which items were legitimate and which were fakes agreed with his personal assessment or not, he knew that all of the valuables that decorated his walls, every last one of them, had been stolen. After all, the thieves had left their calling cards at every heist.

Among the maps, notes, memos, and photographs, dozens of playing cards, most still tucked inside their protective plastic sleeves, were attached to the walls. No matter where he looked, the Queen of Diamonds and the Knave of Spades watched him. The bane of the decade, the thieves who dared to walk into some of the most priceless collections of artworks on the planet and walk back out again with nobody the wiser. Where they had left replicas in place of the items they had stolen, it had taken days, weeks, sometimes even longer to discover the thefts. In fact, he suspected that their burglaries ranged much wider than anyone knew; they simply hadn't been discovered yet.

And so far, nobody had managed to stop them.

He had come close, he knew. Oh, so close. Almost two years ago now, in a desperate maneuver, he and his men had changed tactics completely. Instead of waiting for the pair of felons to strike, he and his men had assembled a list of places that they were likely to hit. The list hadn't been long – only five places, but they had hit pay dirt on one of them.

The Middle Eastern exhibit at the Portland Art Museum had been the perfect opportunity for a stakeout. Some of the most famous pieces from the peak of the ancient Egyptian and Phoenician empires had been brought to one place and opened to the public. His men had spent weeks enhancing the security in the building and working with Christopherson Transport, just in case the thieves attempted a heist while the exhibit was moving from one location to the next.

And it had all been undone, almost, with something as simple and as stupid as a fire.

None of his men had foreseen the fire; it wasn't a tactic the Queen of Diamonds and Knave of Spades had ever used before. Thankfully, deVann already had state-of-the-art tracking chips installed on all of the Christopherson vans so as soon as one of them had deviated from its course, he had been alerted.

His men had been able to recover all of the artifacts stolen during the heist, save one. The photograph of a small, metal bird was tacked up along the west coast of the North American map. As usual, the thieves had escaped, and they had taken a trophy with them.

And then they disappeared.

For weeks, months, deVann had puzzled over their disappearance. Had they come too close to being caught and opted to lie low for a while? He doubted it. If anything, they would have just moved to a new location, possibly even a new country, and started back up again.

But where *were* they?

Wick dropped a file folder in front of him on his desk. It was dark green, which meant it came from the United States Armed Forces. The cover of the folder didn't indicate which branch, but all of them came in the same olive drab folders.

"Looks like we got another hit on them," the junior agent explained as he settled into one of the chairs opposite deVann. "And the Navy's pretty steamed about it."

deVann sighed. He had absolutely no faith that his targets had been involved in a theft from the military, no matter what had been stolen. It wasn't their style. The military didn't have art, they had weapons which, despite their resale value, had never been targeted. "What was taken?"

"Could be one of two things," Wick laughed. "Either there's a pair of people missing, in which case we get to investigate a kidnapping, or the people aren't missing, and we get to investigate a stolen submarine."

deVann looked up from the folder, which he hadn't bothered to open, to see the other man's face. He was slack-jawed, as though he couldn't tell whether his subordinate was serious or not. "We don't *do* kidnappings," he said after a long pause. "Nor do we investigate the Navy's lost sub."

Wick stopped laughing. "Actually," he cleared his throat, "this one might be our people."

deVann doubted that. As hard as he had tried to keep information about the Queen and the Knave out of the news, that many thefts were hard to keep quiet. As soon as the first handful of thefts had been reported, naturally, similar thefts had begun popping up all over the place. None of the perpetrators had been as skillful, or as difficult to apprehend, as the originals, but precious time had been stolen from the task force as they hunted for the copycats.

No matter what he thought, however, it didn't matter. If the case had been assigned to his team by the Department of Defense, he had no choice but to accept it. "Tell me about it." He wanted to hear the brief version first, before reading the file. That made details stick in his mind better and he was able to comprehend what he was reading and connect the details to the ending that he was already aware of.

Kind of like putting a jigsaw puzzle together, really. If you have a clear picture of what the end result was supposed to look like, it made the puzzle easier to put together than one that didn't have a picture.

"Yesterday afternoon," Wick explained, "during a routine inspection of the U.S.S. Virginia, which was about to be launched for its first tour of duty, there was a catastrophic system failure during the dive test."

deVann's eyebrows shot up in surprise. "How did that happen? Those things are tested thousands of times before they're released for duty."

Wick nodded and continued. "According to the report, they aren't really sure what went wrong. They were at about eight hundred feet when the claxons started going off. As per protocol, they tried to blow the ballast tanks to force resurface, but the tanks – the whole system, really - refused to respond."

deVann started to have a sinking feeling in his stomach. He had heard of plenty of submarines that had experienced one type of problem or another, some bad and some worse, but there was something *odd* about what he was hearing. He just couldn't put his finger on what, yet. "So, what happened?"

"There was only a skeleton crew on board," Wick continued. "And the inspectors. The Captain called for all hands to abandon ship, and it sank to the bottom of the Atlantic."

"Of course they sent out a recovery unit."

Wick shook his head. "They did, but the tracking beacon had apparently failed at the same time as the rest of the system crashed. The recovery team went to the last known coordinates of the sub, but there's nothing there."

deVann folded his hands on top of his desk and looked at a pair of playing cards that were tacked to the wall directly next to him. "You mentioned a possible kidnapping." *Innocent until proven guilty, my ass,* he thought. This sounded more and more like something his targets would pull off.

It was certainly audacious enough.

"When the Virginia's crew was retrieved, everyone was returned to the manufacturing facility, where they discovered that two of the inspectors were missing.

"But the best part is," Wick couldn't hide the glint of amusement in his eyes, "those two people weren't even supposed to be on that inspection crew. Nobody in the DoD has any idea who they are."

"Then how did they get there?"

"Someone hacked into the military net, found the schedule for inspections, and added them to the roster. Everything looked completely legitimate until they and the sub were already gone." It was no surprise that Wick had already uncovered the information, everything he lacked in personality he made up in dedication to his job. In fact, it had been Wick's idea of monitoring high-risk targets that had brought the task force the closest they had ever been to catching the Queen and the Knave.

"Yes," deVann nodded. "With the submarine."

He opened the file and skimmed the top page. It was a summary, similar to what Wick had just finished explaining. He turned page after page and saw satellite images of bare water where the submarine had disappeared, partially-redacted schematics of the

U.S.S. Virginia, and photographs and bios for the crew and inspectors who had been recovered.

He stopped and stared at one photo in particular. It showed a tall man and a short woman, neither of whom had biographical information included. What caught his attention most of all was the fact that he recognized the woman.

She had been sitting in his office about eighteen months ago, a witness to the art museum heist. What had her name been?

He tore through other files and papers that were scattered everywhere, searching for one critical piece of information. He hardly breathed, but his heart was pounding in his throat.

They had made a mistake.

He could have howled in triumph as he found the file he was looking for and scattered the papers across his desk. Picking up a handful of worn yellow pages, ripped from one of his thousands of legal pads, he looked up at Wick.

"I need an arrest warrant for Michelle Deva," he said. "And I want to know who all of her known associates are."

Three hours later, his wish was granted. Arrest warrants were issued for Michelle Deva and Thomas Ranger, but it seemed as though those identities had turned into yet another dead end. At the same time as the Queen and Knave had stopped their crime spree, Deva and Ranger had ceased to exist.

And the bad news kept pouring in.

While deVann was waiting for the arrest team to find the fugitives, Wick came in with another briefing from the Department of Defense. "They found the sub," he announced without preamble.

deVann blinked at him, not sure that he had heard the agent correctly. "What do you mean they found it?" They hadn't had time to fake a submarine, had they? Despite how good he knew the pair to be, creating a forgery of an entire sub would take a lot of time, more than the handful of days that had passed since its disappearance.

"The beacon was activated late last night. A recovery team, with SEAL backup, went out to investigate."

They couldn't have just left it out there to be found, could they? deVann wondered. It seemed so far outside the normal range of activities for the people he had been studying that it almost seemed impossible. "Why would they steal something one day, and then leave it out for us to find the next?"

"Like I was saying," Wick continued, "they recovered the submarine, but the nuclear reactor was missing and all of the command controls had been overridden." He dropped a photograph of a pair of playing cards, still in their plastic evidence sheaths, onto his desk. "These were stuck into one of the control panels."

deVann sat back, thunderstruck. He wasn't sure which piece of information was more surprising. Overriding military control codes on a brand-new submarine would take talent that nobody on the planet should possess, but the nuclear reactor appeared to have been their primary target.

What on Earth did they need a nuclear reactor for?

CHAPTER

31

ASSAULT ON CARDISS

Finally.

It had taken over a year, closer to a year and a half, for the plan to be ready and the pieces to be put into place. Each of the ships, with enough crew to run them, was in place. They were scattered at the edges of the Yareth, Zedoin, and Xerxes systems ready to dive in to join the fray as soon as they were needed. More ships, filled with volunteers, were *inside* the Cardiss system.

None of the ships, either the ones inside or the ones stationed outside of Cardiss were expected to do much damage. Not singularly, at least. All of them acting in concert, on the other hand, should have a devastating effect on the King's cards.

It was that *should* that bothered the Queen of Diamonds the most. No matter how many times she went over the plan, no matter how much polishing she did to it, there was always room for chance. She had a handful of contingencies in place to counteract every situation she had thought of that could possibly impact her scheme, but there was always the possibility of something happening that she had not thought of, that she hadn't accounted for.

"It's not too late," Knave said as he looked over, accurately reading the worry on Diamond's face. "We can abort and come up with something else." It wasn't the first time he had reassured her that they didn't need to follow through with the plan, knowing her reticence towards what they were about to undertake.

His words fell on deaf ears, however, as she was determined to do whatever it would take to reclaim ownership of her prized base.

The two of them and their specially-armed ship were powered down in the staging area she had designated behind the rest of their troops. There, they would wait in a holding pattern until the brunt of the attack was well underway. Much as she wanted to lead her people from the front, Knave and Diamond recognized that holding back was necessary. Everyone on the team under-stood the necessity as the ship that they waited in was virtually unarmed.

Knave's reverse EMP cannon had ended up being quite a bit larger than he had expected. As a result, it couldn't be mounted to any of the pre-existing weapons docks. The only place that they had been able to secure the twenty-one-unit-long cannon had been beneath the ship, which had caused them to have to add additional modifications to keep the weapon safe during takeoff and, more importantly, to maintain control of it in the sub-freezing void of space.

Although some members of the Deck had initially believed otherwise, their decision to strip all of the weapon systems from the ship hadn't been an attempt to save weight. In space flight, there was no gravity, and therefore no weight to account for dur-ing the flight and subsequent combat. Other cards had thought that perhaps the weapon removal was due to Diamond's beliefs regarding non-violent actions, but that wasn't the case either.

She recognized the danger that she and Knave, indeed all of their cards, were about to be in and would have felt a lot better if she'd had even some of the most basic weaponry available to her now.

The truth was much simpler and more basic than all of the theories developed by members of the Deck. According to all of Knave's simulations, the electronics from the other weapons had interfered with the reverse EMP weapon. In some tests it had simply failed to fire, but in others it had fired peremptorily, killing the people in the ship it was attached to and everyone in a fourteen-light-year stretch directly in front of it.

The last thing Diamond wanted to do was accidentally kill her own people, and particularly herself and Knave, so she'd put her foot down on the possibility. The ship would be unarmed save for the cannon.

She had foregone her usual attire of short skirts and tall heels in favor of clothing that she felt was less flattering but more suitable for the occasion. Her calves still bare, she wore a pair of green shorts with a golden stripe down the side of either leg. Sturdy boots covered her manicured toes, and a black turtleneck sweater covered the telltale signs of her *tress*. If Knave recognized the meaning of the wardrobe change, he made no comment. After all, it wasn't every day that the Queen of Diamonds sought to cause death. Despite her readiness, she continued to have reservations about their plan.

Instead of answering Knave, she reached for the communication panel and began to activate switches and buttons, bringing the entire screen to life. She opened simultaneous communications with every ship now under her command. All of them would hear her words at the same time.

"We have confirmation," she began, her voice far calmer than she felt. "The last of our ships are in place." She looked up at the screen, where yellow-orange holographic images of each ship floated in mid-air. All she had to do was touch a single one and she would be given every piece of information she needed about the ship, its payload, its specific mission and targets, and the cards inside who operated it.

"Phase One, begin."

Immediately, a third of the holographic ships flashed from yellow-orange to green, indicating that they had changed status from standby to active. On another, larger, monitor next to the communication console, Knave activated the screen that would allow them to watch the beginning stages of the battle as it happened. Rather than the single-position holographic display on Diamond's screen, this one displayed a three-dimensional image taken from multiple points of view. Each ship in their fleet was equipped with viewing cameras, which had all been linked together to offer just such a viewing possibility.

The selected first phase attack ships roared to life, shooting from their stationary positions within the Cardiss system and charging for the main planet. Only moments after the movement began, half of that third dropped their cloaking shields so that they could be seen clearly by any other ships that were in the area.

Almost immediately, intercepting ships moved toward the uncloaked ships. Only seconds after the first phase of the operation began, cards from the King's Deck opened fire on Diamond's ships.

The first, surprised, firefight didn't last very long. The half of the ships Diamond had deployed who were still operating under concealment unleashed weapons of their own on the King's men. Ten, twelve, twenty combative ships fell beneath the overwhelming might of the Queen of Diamond's cards.

Two of her own ships were lost in the battle, but Diamond ignored them. They had been uncloaked and their only purpose had been to act as bait and draw out the enemy fighters. More importantly, that was the reason why none of the visible ships targeted by the King's forces had been occupied. Instead, Knave had been piloting all of them according to a pre-programmed route. Diamond grinned at her partner and flashed him a thumbs-up as the first wave of their invasion went exactly according to plan.

"Phase Two," she spoke into the communication panel again. "Begin."

Another third of the ships shifted into motion, following the initial third as they pushed for Cardiss. This time, Diamond didn't wait for the anticipated counterattack to begin. "Phase Three, begin."

From the far side of Cardiss, more ships rose into view and began to surround the planet. They swarmed the planet like flies on discarded apples, with even more of the traitorous Deck trying desperately to stop their advance.

Ships flickered in and out of view as Diamond called orders to individual units, disorienting and confusing their opponents as the ships they had been firing on – and from which they had been taking fire in return – apparently ceased to exist as new attackers suddenly popped into existence directly behind them. More and more ships were destroyed, mostly from the King's defense but some from Diamond's assaulting force as well. Most of Diamond's lost ships were computer driven, but not all.

Ships belonging to the King of Clubs shattered into frozen fragments under Diamond's relentless onslaught. Some of the manned ships fell as well, and Diamond winced every time a holographic ship flashed to red and then blacked out completely.

She couldn't think about the casualties, she reminded herself. They were gone, and there was nothing she could do to change that. The only thing left was to make sure none of them had died in vain. If she lost the Cardiss base when she was so close, when her people had fought so hard, then their deaths would mean nothing. Meaningful death she could accept when she had to. Meaningless death, on the other hand, was unacceptable.

Finally, when there was enough confusion and debris in the airspace surrounding Cardiss to offer the cover and concealment she needed for the next phase, she nodded to Knave. "Phase Five," she told him without bothering with the communication panel. "Begin."

"On it," he said as another ship on her holographic display flashed from yellow-orange to green. This one didn't bother trying to engage any of the enemy ships. It simply moved forward slowly and carefully toward its ultimate target.

Another drawback that Knave had discovered early on while running his countless simulations, a drawback that he had found no way to counteract, was that the reverse EMP had a surprisingly short effective range. That was the reason why so many other ships had become necessary to their plans; Knave and Diamond had to be almost within visual range of the targeted base in order to guarantee the complete destruction of the electronics it contained.

"All ships," Diamond called as soon as Knave indicated he was within effective range, "power down immediately."

This time, her message was followed by a chorus of confirmations as every light that indicated one of her remaining ships on her holographic display changed from green to blue. As soon as the last of her ships was the correct color, she set her lips into a grim line.

During the battle, one narrow console had been completely ignored by both herself and Knave. It contained none of the communication equipment that Diamond needed to contact her troops. It contained none of the navigation and flight control systems that Knave used while piloting their ship. It contained none of the electronic-relay systems that he had been using to control the first wave of dummy ships.

In fact, this panel only had one small screen that didn't even contain a video display and a single toggle switch under a protective lid to ensure that it wasn't accidentally engaged before it was time. Diamond reached over, activated the panel, and began to align the screen so that their target was the only object visible on it. A simple set of cross-hairs and dimensional coordinates of her target were the only indicators of the events that were about to be put into action. Once the cross-hairs were in the correct position, she locked the screen in place.

"Fire when ready."

With neither confirmation nor reproach, Knave reached over, opened the protective cover, and flipped the toggle switch.

ALL THE KING'S MEN

The base on Cardiss was in a panic. The King of Clubs moved from one Ace to the next throughout his control room, the area of the base where all of the Deck's activity was monitored and security systems were tracked, trying to get someone to tell him what was happening, but he was ignored completely, a response that had become unfamiliar to him during his reign and he didn't like it. Alarms sounded from almost every panel, indicating that something massive was underway, but he had no idea what any of them meant.

"I demand to know what's going on out there," he grabbed onto an Ace, jerking the taller man around to look him in the eye. "You will tell me, or..."

"Your highness," the Ace of Diamonds, part of the King's personal security team, reached between the King and the Heart that he had grabbed. "I'm afraid there's been a bit of an incident. Please allow us to handle it without interference."

As soon as the Ace of Hearts was free, he turned back to running a computer console, toggling switches and adjusting dials, appearing for all the world as though the King's demand hadn't even registered in his ears. He leaned forward and spoke calmly into a microphone, sending commands to the security forces, but in a voice too quiet for the King to overhear, despite standing directly behind.

"What is going on?" the King demanded of his Ace as he was led deeper into the compound. "Why are all the alarms sounding? And why are all my people dressed for battle?" Squads of troops jogged past, all dressed and ready for combat, a visual key that was unmistakable. He hadn't seen such activity since he had first taken control of the base, and its appearance now didn't feel comfortable.

"We're under attack, your highness," the Ace replied smoothly as the lights flickered overhead, "which means we need to get you to safety as quickly as possible." He didn't give the impression that he was concerned in the slightest, despite the words he had just spoken. His footsteps were slow and even as he guided the King down the corridor. "Come along now." His words were more the admonition of a parent to an unruly child than those of a servant to his monarch, but there was no argument forthcoming.

"Attacked? Impossible," the King denied as he followed complicitly. "Nobody would dare..." even as the words escaped into the air, he realized that he was wrong. One person would dare, and he growled as it dawned on him. "It's her, isn't it?"

After his assassination attempt on the Queen of Diamonds had failed, she had stepped up her assault on his control of the Deck. Her people had been wreaking havoc on his cards for months now and he had lost more than a quarter of his men to her growing resistance. Despite all of the spies he had ordered sent to infiltrate her organization, none had reported a single message back to him to indicate her plans. Some reports indicated that the spies he had sent had become traitors, choosing to willingly join her side, but others reported that they had been either killed or apprehended by the ever-present Triad army. None of his Aces, who he had questioned at length over the substantial losses they had taken, had seemed to know any definitive answers, at least, none that they had been willing to divulge to him.

"We aren't sure yet," the Ace responded smoothly as he led him down another corridor and into the King's own suite of rooms. "You'll be perfectly safe here, and I will put extra guards on the door just to be certain of your security."

As the Ace turned to leave, the King stopped and turned back toward the doorway. "Wait," he called after the man. "You can't just leave me in here like this!" If his base was under attack, his suite was one of the most secure areas for him to ride out the invasion but there was no way for him to monitor what was going on or to establish any sort of orders for his people. By remaining hidden in his rooms, he would be completely out of contact with the entire operation.

"Your safety is of the highest priority," the Ace reminded him, overriding his objections. "We cannot allow anything to happen to you."

With that, he closed and sealed the airlock door, leaving the King of Clubs completely alone and with no way to know what was happening outside his apartment.

He could trust his Aces to keep him safe, he was positive about that. He had hand-picked most of them himself, including the Ace of Diamonds, and those he had picked had selected the rest of his elite team. They wouldn't let anything happen to him and they would fight to the last man to keep his base from falling back into the Queen of Diamond's hands.

At least, a small voice in the back of his mind pointed out, he *hoped* they would.

He looked through the small porthole window in the door the Ace had sealed behind him and spotted a handful of guards in the corridor. None of the guards were his personal guard, nor did any of them wear the insignia of Aces, he realized with some surprise. The attack must be going a lot worse than he had thought for all of his Aces, and particularly his personal security team, to be pulled away from guarding him.

With a resigned sigh, he walked into his apartment and flopped onto his couch. There was nothing for him to do and, although he wanted nothing more than to go out and monitor the battle and see how it was going for himself, unless he could find a way to walk through a tenth-unit-thick reinforced space-steel door, he was going nowhere until his Aces returned to retrieve him. He flipped on the entertainment screen, hoping to find something to occupy his attention until it was all over.

And then the lights went out.

They didn't flicker and flash as they normally would if this had been a result of the ongoing battle, or even the brief darkness that would indicate a normal power outage. Everything in the room, from the overhead fluorescent lights to the smaller lamps that one of his frequent girlfriends had referred to as "mood lighting" to the monitor he was looking at flashed more brightly than he had ever seen them before and everything blew at the same time. The darkness was sudden, immediate, and very, very black. In the ensuing silence, he realized that even the air flow system had ceased operation. With the airlock sealed, the only air that entered the room was through the ventilation system that ran on a backup generator to ensure no power outages caused its failure. For it to be silent now indicated that his troubles were much larger and more widespread than he had initially realized.

He stood up from his position on the couch, head cocked as he strained to hear any sounds that would give him information about what was happening, and headed for the door, falling over a low table in the process. Swearing, he pushed himself to his feet and, trying to remember where everything was between where he stood and the only exit, he slowly crept across the room.

A few times he stumbled and almost fell as he tripped over one badly-placed item or another, confused and disoriented in the blackness and silence. At one point, he even slammed face first into a wall he hadn't expected to encounter. When he finally reached the airlock, however, he discovered that his suite was not the only area that had been blacked out.

The corridor beyond the door was a yawning chasm of utter darkness with no discernible shapes. He banged on the glassteel window, shouting for someone to open the door. He pressed his face against the window, trying to see someone, *anyone* on the other side, but was met with only dark silence. Surely the guards who had been placed there to protect him were already working to open the door, weren't they?

With the power out, the King of Clubs recognized how much danger he was in. Without power, it was almost impossible to open any of the airlock doors that kept each wing of the complex secure. The last time he and his Deck had needed to force an airlock, it had taken five men on either side. Since he was the only person on his side of the door and there was nobody on the other side, there was no escape.

He stumbled across his living space until he reached a portal window that gave a glimpse into the space outside. There, he watched as ship after ship abandoned his base and his stomach turned as he realized that without power, not only was there no escape for him, there would soon be no life support. With the critical systems out of commission – however it had happened – the backup power should have automatically started. But there was still no noise to break the oppressive silence.

He walked over to where he believed one of the ceiling vents should be located, waving a hand above his head and searching for the telltale breeze that would give him fresh, breathable air, but there was nothing. No current, no breeze, no motion in the air whatsoever aside from the small vacuum where his hand passed.

Even if the backup generator hadn't started automatically, some-one should have manually engaged it by now, but there was still no response from the ventilation system.

Something had gone seriously, awfully wrong.

Life support failure was about the only thing that could cause the mass evacuation of the base he had seen outside the tiny window. Every space-capable race knew that; many of which learned it the hard way. He understood that because the life sup-port system had obviously failed at the same time as the rest of the power grid had, the cards had to escape.

He just wished that someone would have remembered to see to the safety of their King. Where was his Ace? The Ace of Dia-monds had placed him here for his own protection, certainly he had a plan to keep him alive now, didn't he?

As the minutes ticked silently by, he could tell as his air supply ran low. At first, it seemed as though he couldn't get enough air into his lungs, no matter how many deep breaths he took. He grew weak, and first sat and then lay on the floor. He couldn't remember if there was more or less breathable air closer to the ground, but it didn't matter.

He was going to die.

He was going to die, and it was all his fault.

He recognized his folly. He wasn't really a King, and he hadn't been for a long time. The Ace of Diamonds, his own personally selected guard, had been the one in control the whole time. He had simply been a patsy.

Sure, he had staged the coup and taken over the base, the entire operation, when Diamond had left, but for the first time, he realized why the Queen of Diamonds had never used assassins.

You simply couldn't trust the bastards.

SILENT BASE

The Queen of Diamonds and the Knave of Spades watched through their monitors as the sky darkened around them. They powered down their own ship – not as far as they had directed the others in their fleet to do but enough to keep their own lights from either betraying their position or providing camouflage for anything that was happening below.

The Cardiss base, one that Knave and Diamond had designed and knew every corridor, every room, every maintenance tunnel of, waited before them. From their vantage point, it looked spherical, like a silver ball hovering three thousand units above the surface of the planet, but that view was misleading.

The base was a half-circle, with the flat edge facing Cardiss. There, all of the docking rings were located and the only way to reach them was by entering the atmosphere and curving upwards from beneath the base.

Partly because of the distance from the base to the ground but mostly because Cardiss's atmosphere was comprised primarily of nitrogen, an artificial life support system was mounted in the

very center of the bottom of the base, settled within a slight in-
dentation that would keep it sheltered from any sort of external
attack.

"It looks like all the lights are off," the Tet pointed out, finally
breaking the silence. His face had grown pensive over the last
hour or two, and deep lines were etched into his forehead over all
three of his eyes.

"Yeah," Diamond agreed. She was no less concerned than
Knave, but her face didn't show the worry as easily as his did.
Thankfully, the thick long-sleeved shirt she wore covered her in-
flamed *tress*. "Even the backups seem to be out of commission."

"Looks like we've got action." Knave leaned forward, peering
closely at the monitors. Diamond swiveled her seat to see what
he was watching.

Ships began to emerge from within the base's depths. At first
it was only a few, and then a few more, but soon the sky was filled
with evacuating vehicles. She glanced back at her own monitors
to be sure that all of her ships were still concealed and discovered that most of them had already begun restarting their power
systems and were back online.

"Let them pass," she called out to her team. "We can't take
out all of them right now, but we can deal with them later. For
tonight, let them pass." As she watched the ships fly off in every
direction, she understood that either the standing forces on the
Cardiss base were drastically smaller than she had originally expected or there were still plenty of people trapped on the base
who had not yet made it to evacuation vehicles.

Responses from her own ships came in quickly, most were
agreeable to her direction to hold their fire, but a few of them
sounded disgruntled over it. She made a mental note of which
ships had grumbled the most, reminding her to talk with the
crews later. She had no time to deal with bloodthirsty people.

Using the escaping ships as a cover for their own actions, Knave guided the ship in through the crowd and down toward the swiftly-emptying base. There had been no need to move this close to the planet to launch their attack, but in order to finish the job they would have to be a lot closer. "Ready to breach atmosphere?" he asked over his shoulder.

"Ready as I'm going to get." Diamond tried to alleviate some of her apprehension through laughter, but it came out as a sick-sounding chortle. This next maneuver would be almost as risky as everything else they had done so far in the assault, but there was no point in putting it off any longer. "Let's go."

Bright lights flashed around them as they dropped through the top few layers of atmosphere hovering over the planet. As with most worlds that contained atmosphere, there were multiple layers of air to pass through before they would reach the surface. They traveled through the thermosphere, the mesosphere, stratosphere, and finally into the troposphere before reaching the base. With every layer they flew through, they created a miniature aurora borealis as the magnetism of the planet's surface reacted to the disturbance in its air.

They traveled unmolested to an unoccupied landing dock and, once they were sure the area was clear, headed inside to assess the damage. Both of them wore supplemental oxygen systems, helmets and air tanks strapped to their backs so that they could breathe once inside.

As they had expected, the entire power grid had been knocked offline as a result of the blast from Knave's cannon. Every electronic device that had been powered up or had even been on standby power had been destroyed by their attack, a few consoles still had thin wisps of smoke from the electrical fires that had been a result. Luckily, there didn't appear to be any active fires, one of the possible outcomes that neither of them had been hoping for.

The corridors and rooms were silent as they passed, as though they were entering a tomb. No mechanical noises greeted them, not even the steady hum of a far-off generator. Accustomed to the sounds of living inside an artificial environment as they were, the lack of noise was downright eerie. As both of them wore soft-soled footwear, their steps didn't even cause a whisper to break the ominous hush.

Occasionally the silence was broken by a thunderous noise as an escaping ship took flight. Normally, the distant reverberation of a ship powering up in one of the docking bays would have been muffled by thousands of other, smaller noises and plenty of people moving around, but everything that could have deadened the sound had been taken away already.

There was only one system left in the base that may have survived the reverse EMP cannon's blast, and they headed along familiar corridors toward an old, unused section of the base to locate it.

Long before Diamond and Knave had been exiled, they had upgraded the base's existing systems to a newer StarrTech system that had been designed specifically for atmospheric bases such as the one on Cardiss. Instead of removing the old MicroShield system that had previously been used to power the base, Knave had argued that they should leave it in place.

"You never know when the system will need a backup," he had argued. "Besides, as long as it's turned off, it won't take any extra power." He had always been a fan of redundant backup systems and, while Diamond had thought it to be a foolish gesture, she had acquiesced to his request. Moreover, the expense of removing the outdated system had been more than she had been willing to pay at the time.

Today, Diamond was glad she had agreed to go along with his recommendation. What had initially begun as a silly whim, the overly-cautious desires of her partner and best friend, now became the difference between regaining control of her home base and abandoning it forever.

They reached the control room, filled with the massive heart of the StarrTech system, and began pulling panels away from the back wall of the room. There, hidden for years behind a thin layer of paneling, waited the old, archaic system that Knave had fought so hard to save.

She had never been so happy that Knave was a firm believer not just in brand-new technology, but in old technologies as well.

Now, perhaps, it would save them all.

Fifteen minutes after walking into the room, basic life support systems were active. Slowly, lights began to flicker on some of the control panels. Diamond was amazed that the fifty-year-old system had started as easily as it had. They just didn't make things like that anymore.

"Okay," Knave conceded. "It's not as good as the new system. This won't support much for very long."

"Long enough to start getting some of this damage repaired," Diamond retorted flippantly. "And right now, that's all that matters." She settled her pack onto the ground near the StarrTech system and accepted Knave's pack as well. Both of them had been carrying packs of replacement circuit breakers, pieces of hardware that controlled the flow of electricity to the power system. Although their replacement wouldn't turn everything back on, it would allow her to assess how much damage the system had received during the attack and figure out what else would need to be repaired or replaced. From what she understood of the StarrTech system, which she had spent the last month researching, it was supposed to have contained an internal safety monitoring system that should have turned the whole thing off before too much damage had occurred, but she would have no way of knowing how well those safeties had worked until she restored power to it.

To her relief, there was almost no damage to the system itself, although many of the subsidiary systems that were controlled by it would have to be manually restarted in order to return to full operation. When there had been no sounds of takeoff from any of the landing ports for well over half an hour, she and Knave finally gained full control over the base's systems. As they began restoring power, Diamond didn't want to take any chances.

"One system at a time," she explained. "I want to search each section as it comes back online." When he looked at her doubtfully, she explained. "Not physically, that would be insane. I want to run a bioscan as soon as the system's active to look for life signs."

She didn't have to voice her fears. She knew how unlikely it was that any of the King's cards had remained on the base after evacuation, although she knew that if they used portable life support like she and Knave were using, they very well could have. The last thing she wanted was any surprise visitors.

The first five decks were activated without incident and the bioscan searches turned up absolutely nothing. The sixth one, on the other hand, showed that there was indeed something alive on one of the outer edges of the complex.

Once the base was completely under their control, Diamond and Knave went to the wing where the life sign had been. A young man with long black hair, younger than either Diamond or Knave, was lying on the floor beyond a sealed airlock door. A steady breeze blew into the finely-decorated corridor, but he hadn't yet regained consciousness.

"He's got to be one of them," Diamond evaluated the situation. "This doesn't look like a wing where they would keep prisoners."

Knave nodded his agreement. "What do you want to do with him?"

"Open the door." She could barely see through the small window, which was placed a bit too high in the door for her comfort.

"He might still be alive." A hissing noise preceded the movement of the door, so she backed away before anything got caught in its motion.

As soon as there was enough room to squeeze through, she darted into the all-but-deserted hallway and reached for the young man's throat. "He's still alive," she called over to Knave as she felt the weak pulse.

Because she had respect for life, despite the owner of the life in question, she had Knave carry the boy to the medical wing so that he could be treated for whatever injuries he was suffering from besides oxygen deprivation. Because she was not a fool, she bound him to the bed with restraints until they could discover who he was and how much of a danger he would pose to them.

Gleefully, she and Knave skipped along familiar corridors and threw open doors to familiar rooms on their way back to the command center. The King of Clubs and his cards had changed a lot in the base during her absence, but she was pleased to see that none of the damage seemed to be permanent.

Okay, she skipped. He jogged to keep up with her.

"Come on in," she called out over the communication panel as soon as they arrived back in the command center.

"It's time to come home."

Keep reading for an exclusive sneak peek at

Worth More Dead: Shadow Tribunal, book 2

Available November, 2024

The air was thick and heavy, smothering in the blackness that surrounded M'Tarl. As she slowly came to consciousness, she realized that it wasn't just the air that was thick and heavy, there was something pressing tightly around her. Only the smallest pocket of air had granted her enough room to continue breathing. Confused and uncertain of how she had arrived in this strange situation, she tried to look around, but the dirt held her tightly.

"Buried?" she asked herself quietly as she determined how bad of a situation she was in. She spat out a mouthful of dirt, realizing that opening her mouth while underground wasn't the wisest of decisions. "That's a new one for me, I haven't been buried before. I guess I should just be thankful they hadn't chosen a more creative method of body disposal." She reached out with her senses, confused when she got nothing in return. Not even the slightest trace of life filtered through her mind, something she had never experienced before except in the furthest reaches of space.

Immediately her mind turned to probable situations in which she might currently find herself. Her absolute worst-case situation, but given the lack of psionic response was the most likely one, was that she had been encased in a box of dirt and then jettisoned out into space. If that was the case, then she was dead regardless of what actions she may take. Since that option had no hope of survival, she turned her attention to the more survivable, of less likely, options before her. She had to be either in the same dirt-filled box that she had just imagined floating around in space, only this time above ground, or had been buried, coffin-less, underground. Of the possibilities, she liked the idea of having been buried without a coffin the most, as it had the highest chance of survival.

She just hoped that she had been buried neither too deep nor under something solid, because the meager air pocket she had available wouldn't last for much longer. Since she had been unconscious when placed into this particular position, she had no clue how long she had been out but she was thankful that she had woken before the air was depleted entirely. As she began to dig her way out, her entire body began to scream in pain, causing her to stop every so often to rest, but she had no time to relax. If she didn't reach air soon, the grave would become permanent. Just the movements she had already made had caused the air pocket to collapse under the moving dirt. She gritted her teeth and continued to dig, pushing aside the pain that screamed through her body.

Three minutes later, she reached the surface and took in a deep breath of clear air, coughing out some loose grains of soil that had found themselves in places they didn't belong. Only the rigorous training she had undergone early in her career had allowed her to remain calm during her escape, as moving while suffocating would have induced immediate panic in most people. She, on the other hand, was hardly like most people. After a few more breaths, she took a look around to figure out not only where she was but also where to go from there.

She was in an area thick with trees and no sounds of life nearby. After pulling herself the rest of the way out of the ground, she lay on the grass next to her grave, enjoying the presence of fresh air. The memories of all that had transpired, leading up to her untimely burial, and thoughts of those who believed her dead flickered through her mind, but she shoved them aside. She had more important things to attend to than to search for people who were certainly long gone. After all, this wasn't the first time M'Tarl had been left for dead and, given her career, it was unlikely to be the last.

Briefly very concerned, she tapped her chest, relieved to discover that her most precious item, the small silvery ring, was still hanging by its chain in place around her neck.

She reached out with her senses to find the closest inhabited area and frowned in confusion when she found nothing. There were no detectable thought patterns within her radius of effect, which meant that either she was much further away from civilization than she had first realized or there was something substantially wrong. Her psionics had never failed her before and she wondered what her captors had done to her once she had lost consciousness for them to cease working in this way.

Glancing around, she appreciated the serenity of the clearing in which she had been buried. "At least you picked a nice spot for me," she conceded. "Might have been nice had you waited just a little longer before putting me here, though." She winced again as she pushed herself to her feet, wondering how extensive the damage was. Covered in earth as she was, she wouldn't be able to see the extent of the damage so she didn't bother trying.

With a little luck, there would be a stream or some other source of clear water nearby that she could use to cleanse her wounds and prevent the infection that she was sure had already begun to spread throughout her body. Dirt was hardly the optimal poultice for open wounds. Staying put wasn't an option, so she had no other choice. She picked a direction and began to walk. She stumbled only a few times, sore muscles and open wounds protesting loudly against the forced march but she ignored all of it.

The sun was beginning to glint from the treetops an hour later, an orange glow washing over the horizon as the skies turned pink and blue, indicating the advent of sunrise, when M'Tarl spotted the edge of a town. She reached out her senses again, knowing for certain that someone had to be within her range, but still received no information in return. Her brows furrowed in confusion. She could see visually that there were people waking and heading out into their morning business, but she couldn't hear a single thought from any of them. Either these people had suddenly gained some sort of psychic defenses that they hadn't possessed the previous day or there was something else blocking her from hearing them. Something had definitely gone wrong.

Thankfully, she recognized the town. She had personally landed her ship just beyond the sleepy little residential area, so as long as it was still there, clean water and bandages awaited her.

There was nothing more for her to do in the area so she made short time moving past the houses and other assorted buildings to reach the parking area.

Her ship, a small cruiser, waited exactly where she had left it, a great relief. Part of her mind had been convinced that the people who had buried her had also taken possession of it, leaving her without easy egress from the area. While she harbored no ill will towards the townspeople, she had little interest in remaining planetside any longer than necessary, at least on that planet. Should her would-be murderers discover her empty grave, they would certainly come in search of her and she intended to be as far away as possible before that could happen. Even more so now since she couldn't sense them coming. Being blindsided was not a prospect to which she was used and she had no intention of giving anyone such an advantage, particularly those who wished her dead.

The first thing she did after powering the ship on was to engage the active camouflage, unwilling to draw any further attention to herself during takeoff. Although small craft such as hers were common in the skies above, an observant onlooker may notice her departure, also low on her list of things she wanted to happen. The autopilot engaged as soon as she was in orbit and she set the destination to the last planet she had been on where she knew she would be safe.

After life growing up in the beautifully rainy Pacific Northwest, Shanon L. Mayer tends to keep indoors, writing story after story, building vivid worlds on paper while her thoughts hold everything but images. She tends to look at everything in her world for inspiration – especially her collections of skulls, dragon statues, swords and knives, and pretty much anything that fits her eclectic, geeky-gothic lifestyle.

When her busy life feels like too much, she can be found relaxing with a hot mug of tea and a documentary on anything from theoretical physics to deep ocean wildlife to the most famous heists the world has ever seen.

Milton Keynes UK
Ingram Content Group UK Ltd.
UKHW042037081123
432235UK00012B/173/J